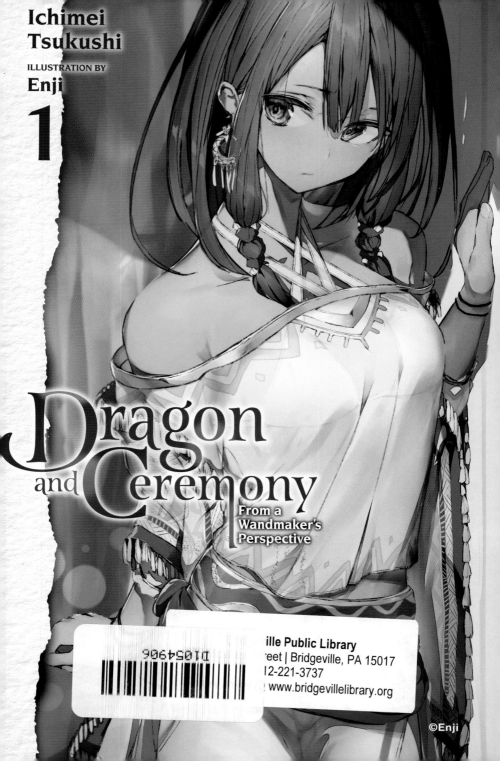

Ichimei
Tsukushi

ILLUSTRATION BY
Enji

1

Dragon
and Ceremony

From a
Wandmaker's
Perspective

©Enji

CONTENTS

PROLOGUE · **Dance of Dust** ———— 001

CHAPTER 1 · **A Wand in Hand** ———— 011

CHAPTER 2 · **Book-Laden** ———— 051

CHAPTER 3 · **Towering Bonfire** ———— 109

CHAPTER 4 · **Look Toward the Summit** — 165

EPILOGUE · **Rising Stars** ———— 223

DRAGON AND CEREMONY

Presented by Ichimei Tsukushi

Yuui

Wand-repair client.

©Enji

Ottou

Child prodigy.

Ix

Novice wandmaker.

Morna

Former apprentice, senior to Ix. Like a sister to him.

Dragon and Ceremony

From a Wandmaker's Perspective

1

Ichimei Tsukushi

ILLUSTRATION BY **Enji**

YEN ON

New York

DRAGON AND CEREMONY
ICHIMEI TSUKUSHI

Translation by Jordan Taylor
Cover art by Enji

RYU TO SAIREI Vol. 1 -MAHOUJOUSHOKUNIN NO KENCHI KARA-
Copyright © 2020 Ichimei Tsukushi
Illustrations copyright © 2020 Enji
All rights reserved.
Original Japanese edition published in 2020 by SB Creative Corp.

This English edition is published by arrangement with SB Creative Corp., Tokyo
in care of Tuttle-Mori Agency, Inc., Tokyo.

English translation © 2022 by Yen Press, LLC

Yen On
150 West 30th Street, 19th Floor
New York, NY 10001

Visit us at yenpress.com
facebook.com/yenpress
twitter.com/yenpress
yenpress.tumblr.com
instagram.com/yenpress

First Yen On Edition: January 2022

Yen On is an imprint of Yen Press, LLC.
The Yen On name and logo are trademarks of Yen Press, LLC.

Library of Congress Cataloging-in-Publication Data
Names: Tsukushi, Ichimei, author. | Enji, illustrator. | Taylor, Jordan (Translator),
   translator.
Title: Dragon and ceremony / Ichimei Tsukushi ; illustration by Enji ;
   translation by Jordan Taylor.
Other titles: Ryū to sairei. English
Description: First Yen On edition. | New York, NY : Yen On, 2022–
Identifiers: LCCN 2021046140 | ISBN 9781975336936 (v. 1 ; trade paperback.) |
   ISBN 9781975336950 (v. 2 ; trade paperback) | ISBN 9781975336974 (v. 3 ;
   trade paperback)
Subjects: CYAC: Fantasy. | Dragons—Fiction. | Quests (Expeditions)—Fiction. |
   LCGFT: Fantasy fiction. | Light novels.
Classification: LCC PZ7.1.T7826 Dr 2022 | DDC [Fic]—dc23
LC record available at https://lccn.loc.gov/2021046140

ISBNs: 978-1-9753-3693-6 (paperback)
       978-1-9753-3694-3 (ebook)

10 9 8 7 6 5 4 3 2 1

LSC-C

Printed in the United States of America

Ix felt a twinge of emptiness as he left the shop. The feeling was perfectly understandable, but it nevertheless surprised him. As if drawn in by the emotion, he turned back toward the entrance.

It was empty inside.

Old shelves lined the walls. The furniture in the back room and on the second floor had been left behind. If the next resident needed them, they were welcome to help themselves. Otherwise, they could break down the furnishings for firewood.

Ix wondered if a buyer would ever show up. This was a declining village in the middle of the mountains, after all. But he'd be in quite the predicament if no one purchased it. His adoptive father was now gone, and Ix had no job lined up in his absence. The little money he had to his name could cover his living expenses for the time being, but not much else.

A ray of light shone into the shop through the slightly cracked door, illuminating the swirling dust.

Suddenly, Ix recalled his teacher's coarse voice.

"*Do you know what happens to your body after you die in Marayist scripture?*" asked the man, withered like an old tree.

He lay on a pallet bed on the floor, his face turned toward Ix as he desperately tried to string words together. He was certain he would die when his words stopped coming.

"*They say your soul exits from your mouth, then soars up to heaven—was that it?*" said the man.

"*That's right.*" Ix nodded indifferently.

"*Hmph, I don't believe that drivel. The world isn't, hmm, isn't so convenient.*"

"*So what happens when you die, then?*"

"*I'll turn to dust.*"

"*Dust?*"

"*Living things expand when they die. Get so huge you can't see 'em. And they grow so light, so weightless, that they turn to dust and scatter all over.*" The man spoke in a single breath before letting out a cough that was like a breeze passing through trees.

"*Floating about sounds nice and carefree.*"

"*Carefree, huh?*" His teacher's lips trembled. "*And what's left after that? A half-baked craftsman like you? How's that reassuring?*"

"*You've got plenty of other excellent apprentices.*"

"*Ah, no. No, no. There's no hope for them and wandmaking. What a disaster for my clientele...*"

His voice gradually faded. Then his breathing finally slowed, and he nodded off.

As his death drew nearer, the old man alternated between lengthy rests and delirious ramblings. His naps grew longer and longer, until one day he didn't wake again. This had happened a month ago.

Ix remembered all this while staring at the dust flitting about inside the room.

"So even the legendary wandmaker Munzil turns to dust when he dies?" The words fell from Ix's tongue before he closed the door.

A sign no longer hung outside the shop. The only vestige of the place were the words *Putting wands in the right hands* carved into the wood of the entrance.

Since the shop was located on the edge of the village, Ix managed to leave without passing any other residents. He gently shifted the luggage he carried. It was still early in the morning. The sun was only half visible, just beginning to warm the cool earth.

First, he was planning to go to Leirest, a city to the south. Even on foot, he should arrive before sunset.

After passing the beast-warding fence, Ix stood at the entrance to the village. Just then, he saw someone he didn't recognize. A lone figure was trailing up the road that led south. Their whole body was cloaked in a gray coat, face hidden below a hood.

Though Ix was about to bid it farewell, this was the village he'd grown up in. Thus, a shred of obligation to his hometown kept him waiting by the gate. He would have to warn everyone if a suspicious character was coming this way.

Soon, they stood face-to-face.

The other person was about a head shorter than Ix. Their coat was made of fairly high-quality material. Despite their expensive-looking clothing, they didn't have an attendant to carry their things for them; instead, they'd hoisted a large bag across their back. Everything about this traveler seemed contradictory. Ix couldn't make out their face beneath the shadow of their hood.

For a brief moment, the two figures faced each other in silence.

"Um," came a female voice from beneath the hood. Her voice was somewhat deep. "Is there a wand shop here?" she asked.

"A wand shop?"

"I've been told there was one in this village."

"...Ah." Ix nodded slightly.

I see—she must have come to check it out.

Since there was no one in the village to buy the building, they'd sent word of its sale to the towns at the base of the mountains. The woman could be a potential buyer who'd arrived to examine the shop before purchasing, or perhaps she was someone who worked in real estate. Ix couldn't imagine what value she'd seen in this out-of-the-way location, however...

Either way, she was his customer. He should be kind.

"Head into the village, and it'll be the first building you see," he informed her.

"Thank you."

With that, she disappeared into town.

"…She going to open a store?"

Ix sighed. As much as he didn't want to, he'd have to start putting himself out there from today on. All he had at the moment were a few coins and his skill as a wandmaker.

About twenty years ago, Ix had been abandoned outside that store—Munzil's wand shop. There hadn't even been a note left alongside him, just a baby wrapped in rags dumped on the doorstep. It had been snowing that day.

Munzil had gone outside to get water when he saw the baby boy, then took him in and raised him by himself. He named the baby Ix, which meant *snow*.

Everyone in town was taken aback. Munzil was a famous craftsman renowned throughout the kingdom for both his peerless wandmaking skills and his stubbornness. No one ever imagined he would pick up a child and, of all things, raise him as his kin.

Perhaps he'd seen his own impending death coming.

Eventually, that child became Munzil's last apprentice, as all his others had long since left. Ix had been the only one there when the craftsman had finally passed.

Per Munzil's wishes, they hadn't held a funeral. The kingdom's most celebrated wandmaker moved on from this world quietly. His crafting materials and documents had been taken care of before he'd died, and in accordance with his will, the wand shop had been shuttered. He'd disappeared without a trace, as though he were dust in the wind. Now, all that remained of Munzil were tales of his exploits and the apprentices he'd trained…

Ix came to a halt. Wiping the sweat from his brow, he looked up to the sky. The sun had reached its zenith. A strong breeze blew up the slope, tousling his hair. He decided to take a break and sat down on the edge of the road.

Esne trees continued endlessly into the distance on either side of the path. Their leaves were sharp, and their bark was hard. Since they repelled magic, they weren't suited for making wands. But they did prevent magic beasts from entering the village. By this same token, many cities had either planted esne forests or constructed fences made from esne wood around their borders.

Long ago, this trail had served as the main artery between the cities of the area because it had been cleared out from a naturally occurring esne forest. Apparently, the villages along the road had prospered from travelers stopping there for lodging.

However, the construction of Kusa Zuf, the royal highway, about fifty years ago had made the meandering path redundant. The short weeds growing along the road were testament to how few pedestrians it had these days.

When Ix stood up from his rest, he heard the rustle of approaching footsteps in the grass.

Looking back, he saw the woman from this morning briskly striding toward him. She held her hood with one hand against the wind to keep it in place.

She must have finished checking out the shop already.

As Ix thought about how busy the merchant world must be, the woman came to a stop before him.

Her shoulders were heaving, and her breath was ragged; she'd probably rushed over here.

Still out of breath, she shouted, "Why did you lie to me?"

Ix was confused. "The location I told you should have been correct."

"The shop is not there anymore!"

"The owner died."

"What...? Why didn't you tell me that earlier?"

"You didn't ask."

"No one at the foothills could tell me whether he was alive or dead. Apparently, there hasn't been a funeral."

"Unfortunately, there won't be one. Is that what you came here to confirm?"

"No, it's not!" she shouted, clenching her fists with rage. When she let go of her hood, the wind filled it and pushed it back.

Black hair tinged with blue spilled out, followed by brown skin. A decorative earring on her right ear made a metallic jingle. Her young face proved that she was clearly not quite an adult yet.

She looked surprised for a moment, but that quickly gave way to anger.

"A kid?" muttered Ix to himself. Then he asked her, "Where did you come from?"

"The capital."

"All the way in the mountains?"

"I wouldn't be able to get it if I didn't leave."

"Get what?"

Her sharp gaze pierced Ix. She pointed her finger at him. "*You*, wandmaker."

"You've got it all wrong."

"Huh? Are you not Ix?"

"I am. Who are you?"

"My name is Yuui," she announced, holding a hand to her chest. "But you really *are* Ix, correct?"

"I am."

"I heard from the villagers. The shop owner died, and his apprentice is heading toward Leirest today."

"Yeah, that's me, but I'm no wandmaker. I'm not registered with the Guild."

"Huh, uh, what...?" She looked bewildered. She must not have known about the guild system. Based on her appearance, she was probably from the east. Now that he thought about it, he realized her speech did sound somewhat stiff, but she was so fluent in Central Standard, you wouldn't notice if you weren't paying close attention.

"Falsely claiming to be a craftsman if you're not registered

©Enji

with the Guild is a crime. As of right now, I'm just an apprentice—except I'm not even that, strictly speaking. No shop would hire me," he admitted.

"Y-you cannot fool me," said Yuui, shaking her head. "Apprentice or not, you are involved with Munzil's store, yes?"

"That's right."

"S-so you finally admit it. Now I won't let you get away."

"I said as much from the beginning. No one's running here," Ix deadpanned. He met Yuui's glare with a blank expression.

"All right, what business do you have with someone connected to Munzil?" he asked.

"I-if you'd only been honest with me from the start..."

"I get it. Tell me what you want."

"Urgh... You better not regret asking." She slid a hand into her coat and brought out a wand. "Fix this!"

"I can't."

"Huh, w-wait, at least take a moment to consider..."

"I told you before, I'm not a craftsman. It's a crime for a non-craftsman to do business. Even just a repair," he said carefully, staring at the wand.

Technically, a wandmaker worked with both wands and staffs. Staffs were about as tall as a person, while wands tended to be the length of your elbow to your fingertips. They were otherwise the same, though the length affected their durability and spell output rate. The longer the staff, the more durable it was. On the other hand, the wand Yuui had pulled out was a standard type. Those excelled at quick spellcasting.

There was a common saying about when to use a wand versus when to use a staff: Wands for person against person, staffs for army against army. There was also a joking rhyme that went along with it: Use a wand once a day, then throw away. Use a staff every day, for it will always obey.

Regardless, the wand Yuui held was a masterpiece like none Ix had ever seen.

The wood was most likely five-hundred-year-old nueb. It was nearly black in hue, discolored from significant use. An antique. Despite its age, the wand's smooth form barely showed any signs of warping. In terms of value, Ix figured a minor noble would be able to purchase it only if they sold everything they owned.

"Did Munzil make that wand?" he asked.

"Y-yes. Do you recognize it?"

"No, I've never seen it. Must have been from before my time."

"You say that like you remember every wand he's made since then."

"I do."

"Wha…?" She stared at Ix, her eyebrows furrowed.

While any wand was hard to come by, it was almost impossible for citizens of the kingdom to get their hands on ones his teacher had made.

So why did this girl have one…?

Even if this area was pretty close to a major city, it was also very strange for someone from the east to travel all the way out to the kingdom's mountains.

"Wh-what?!" Yuui cried out when she noticed Ix eyeing her suspiciously. "Anyway, don't think I'll let you get away if you try to flee," she asserted. "I have a contract."

"A contract?"

"Yes. A promise to repair the wand."

"I'm not bound by promises."

"Even if you are not," said Yuui as she searched in her bag before pulling out an old envelope, "your master is."

"That's what it says?"

"So I've been told."

Frowning, Ix snatched the envelope.

The seal was definitely Munzil's. There was no doubt that his teacher wrote this. Inside the envelope was a single small sheet of paper.

On the honor of the name of Munzil Alreff, it is declared that any maintenance on this wand (engraved number: 8305, Smooth) shall be completed once without fee, if requested within the following three hundred years.

Furthermore, it will be guaranteed that if this should occur after the death of Munzil, this contract will be fulfilled by one of his craftsman apprentices.

To the first one reading this, that would be you, you simpleton. Do not dare to ever touch a wand again if you abandon this task.

It looked as though Ix's teacher had returned surprisingly quickly as something far heavier, bigger, and, most important, more bothersome than dust.

CHAPTER 1 — A Wand in Hand

1

By the time the sun began to set, they could see the walls of Leirest. Even though the city was nowhere near the kingdom's border, its barriers were heavily fortified because it was a main travel hub. Since they were currently at a higher elevation, Ix and Yuui could just about peer into the city. It was packed with roofs, not a single space left between.

"Aah, I'm so hungry..."

Ix looked back at Yuui, who followed on unsteady feet. They'd arrived later than he'd hoped because he'd had to match his pace to hers. According to what she told him on the way here, she'd arrived in Leirest the previous evening, which meant she'd walked for basically an entire day. She hadn't eaten since having dinner on her way to Ix's village; no wonder she was running out of energy. On top of that, she'd probably been on edge the whole time because she was on a mountain path at night. That would've added to her fatigue.

Ix waited for Yuui to catch up, then told her, "This path's protected from magic beasts, but we're still in the mountains, you know. There are plenty of garden-variety creatures here that'll see you as nothing more than a meal."

"The moon was out last night, so I decided it was not danger-ous. Also, I was planning on purchasing food at the village, but you made me rush 'cause you were being so inconsiderate."

"I don't remember saying anything out of line."

"You just…do not have any manners, do you?"

"Master never taught me how to interact with the customers."

"Can you be a craftsman without that?"

"I'm actually one of the more likable of his apprentices."

"Huh?"

Once the two of them made their way down the mountain, the trail merged with Kusa Zuf. The path underfoot was now cobblestone.

Farm fields enclosed by a simple wooden fence stretched out a short way from the edge of the road.

"That's surprising," muttered Ix.

"What is?" asked Yuui.

"The fields have gotten a lot bigger since the last time I came here."

"Is that so? I only just arrived, so I wouldn't know." Yuui nod-ded. "Good to see they are so diligent."

"I wonder…"

"Is something bothering you?"

There had been a surprising amount of distance to cover from the point when they'd first glimpsed the walls of their destina-tion; by the time they'd reached the gates of Leirest, the sun had already dipped behind the city skyline.

The massive gates were still open. Guards stood on either side, glaring threateningly at the people coming and going. Occa-sionally, they would demand merchants and travelers stop for a moment before checking their piles of goods.

Ix produced his travel pass from his shirt and hung it from his neck so it was visible. Yuui did the same but put her hood up again.

"Hold on, you two!" shouted a bearded guard just as they were about to pass through the gate. Ix immediately stopped and stared at him. The other travelers halted as well, looking similarly anxious.

The man strode over briskly and passed Ix to stand before Yuui. He was about Ix's height, so he really towered over her.

"Show your face," he demanded.

"Do you mean me?" replied Yuui.

"That's right. Hurry up."

"I..."

"Hey, don't worry," reassured the guard, his tone suddenly turning soft. "It's just a precaution. You got a pass, no one's gonna stop you 'cause of your face."

"...All right." Yuui lifted her hood and cast her eyes down, her tanned skin and blue-tinged black hair now visible.

"Huh...?" The guard cocked an eyebrow. "An early delegate?"

"No," replied Yuui.

"Of course not, not a kid like you... Hey, let me see your pass again," he demanded, tugging on the pass Yuui still had in her grip. The action pulled her up on her toes, and she grimaced as her neck muscles craned. A laugh rose from the circle of travelers surrounding them. It was impossible to tell who it came from.

After examining the pass for a while, the guard suddenly released it. Yuui teetered but managed to regain her footing without falling.

"Eh, whatever. You can go," said the guard.

"Thank you."

"Just don't get into trouble, 'cause if anything happens to someone like you, we ain't gettin' involved."

"...Of course."

"Hey, the rest of you, don't stand here blocking the gate!"

The travelers started up again as though they'd suddenly

remembered how to move, but now things were different. This time, there were whispers about Yuui mixed into the chatter of the crowd.

Covering her face with the hood again, Yuui moved forward and kept her eyes on the ground. Ix watched her.

He didn't really know how people from the east were treated in the kingdom. People from all walks of life used to visit the shop, but nobody had ever told him outright what it was like for them. Besides, this was actually the first time he'd met someone from the east. But based on how the guard had harassed her and the reactions of the crowd, Ix wasn't getting the impression they were greatly welcomed.

As they passed through the gate, Yuui whispered, "Let's go, Ix."

"Yeah," he said with a shrug.

Leirest was busy even in the evening.

It had originally expanded as a trade city, but since Kusa Zuf's construction, it had become a gathering point for people and goods flowing in and out of the kingdom and grown even more prosperous. In fact, its economic activity and population had risen so consistently that there were now enough people crammed between its walls to make you feel as if you were suffocating.

Merchant after merchant called out to Ix and Yuui as they made their way down the street. Everything was on offer, from food to gems to fabrics spread on the road. Yuui stopped momentarily in front of a merchant who'd set out some tools with strange patterns on them.

"Hey, you, with the face I can't see! Here we have items exhumed from the disposal grounds of indigenous religions, of gods long dead in this kingdom, and..." Without missing a beat, the merchant launched into a fishy spiel. Yuui hastily pulled her hood down farther and strode away. Ix remained completely expressionless as he passed by the merchant.

Tired of the crowd, the pair stepped into an alleyway, only to be hit with a horrible stench halfway down. Garbage and detritus were scattered everywhere.

"...We're going this way?" asked Yuui, looking unhappy.

"Personally, I prefer real trash to human trash. If you don't like it, you can take a different route, though."

"I—I will stay with you," she said, following him so closely, she was almost clinging to his back. Ix wondered why she was forcing herself if it bothered her that much.

"By the way, where are we headed?" asked Yuui.

"A wand shop."

"A-are you off-loading me onto them? But you promised to fix it..."

"I am accepting the responsibility as promised. I'll fix it. But I need tools and materials to do it. And before that, I've got to examine the wand in detail. I can't do that by myself. Not without specialized equipment."

"I take it you know someone, then?"

"There's this lady—she was another one of my master's apprentices. Since he left this job behind, she won't refuse to assist us."

"This lady... Is she as dreadful as you are?"

"She's highly capable."

"Capable, huh...?" mumbled Yuui, placing a hand on her cheek as she thought. "But is there really a wand shop here? I did search this city fairly thoroughly to locate someone who would fix mine."

"First I've heard of that. You couldn't find anyone?"

"W-well, I was told that just examining the wand would cost quite a bit of money... And while it was unclear whether your master was alive, I had the contract, so I opted to go there first...," explained Yuui, looking down in embarrassment.

A wand as high quality as that needed to be handled delicately, so the craftsman had probably requested an additional fee to cover the difficulty of the job. Buying a good tool took some serious cash, and using it for a long time required even more. You could even argue a tool was only as good as the money you put into it.

Following his memory of the area, Ix turned a corner. As they were about to leave the alley, something moved at his feet.

"Eeeek!" Yuui let out a brief shriek and hid behind Ix.

They saw some rags squirming down at the edge of the road. Ix initially suspected a large rat or a stray cat, but that wasn't it. Sprouting out from beneath the rags were a pair of arms and legs with dull skin.

It was a human.

A thin, starving homeless person sat on the edge of the road. They stared into the space with lifeless eyes.

Ix and Yuui quickly went elsewhere but soon ran into a number of other people in similar situations. One was curled up in a ball, while another begged from passersby with a withered outstretched hand. The area was overflowing with starving masses, regardless of age or gender.

"The people in this alley are too weak to go beg on the main street," murmured Ix. "If there're this many here, how many are there in the entire city...?"

"The capital wasn't nearly this bad..."

"It wasn't this desperate when I came a few years ago, either. I've heard stories that the capital doesn't have many homeless people—is that true?"

"There are a few, of course, but most are taken to an almshouse or given work. The rest scrape by through begging."

"The current king is apparently big on antipoverty initiatives; he must be working on it close to home first."

In places beyond the king's reach, however, unhoused people were simply ignored. Even if folks wanted to help them, the funds weren't there. Given Leirest's reputation as a commercial hub, it seemed obvious that raising taxes to help the poor would be a controversial idea. Other cities would be much the same. Places where Marayism was strong might be another story, though...

Yuui sighed glumly as she walked beside Ix. "I had heard the kingdom was prosperous," she said.

"It is. The increase of homeless people just means the population is increasing accordingly."

"That does not matter if there are more citizens in poverty, though. Why is there this unrestrained growth?"

"Dunno. Might be a rebound effect."

"Rebound from what?"

"You heard of the sonim plague?"

"Yes, I am aware of it."

An epidemic of sonim, an illness sometimes called the broken-mind sickness, had swept the kingdom about twenty years ago and wiped out nearly a third of its population. The plague pushed it to the brink of collapse. And it wasn't confined to the kingdom, either; the disease also spread to neighboring countries and similarly devastated them.

Although Ix had grown up in a tiny mountain hamlet, he knew a lot about the topic, having learned from his master's customers who came to visit.

He began to explain, prefacing to Yuui that everything he knew about the plague he'd heard secondhand.

"Since sonim killed so many people regardless of status, commoners and aristocrats alike, it weakened the grip of the nobility. Serfs gained money and freedom. Some peasants even managed to save up small fortunes. As a result, those people started having lots and lots of children. The kingdom's population exploded, and it keeps going up to this day. Supposedly, that's why the kingdom recovered a bit faster than the surrounding nations. With a larger population, you've got more people to work."

"But how would that result in there being more people in poverty as well?"

"That's simple. Food shortages," explained Ix, shaking his

head. "The number of people in an area increases, but the amount of food to go around doesn't. That's why the cost of groceries is on the rise. Some people have so little to eat, they stoop to begging. When their family scatters, they have nowhere to go, so their only option is sleeping on the side of the street. It looks like they're scrambling to increase the amount of arable land right now, but...I don't think they can catch up, especially when you consider how easily populations can grow."

Yuui nodded in understanding, though all Ix could see was her hood moving slightly.

"Then why don't they employ the poor to assist in expanding farmland?" she asked.

"There's only so much land to work with," replied Ix immediately. "Get it? They're now having to go into areas that were previously unsuitable for agriculture."

"Because of poor soil?"

"There's that, but the biggest roadblock is magic beasts."

"...Ah, I see." Yuui sighed. "So what you are saying is that any acreage that has not been converted to farmland is infested with magic beasts. They try to expand agriculture but are unable. There are few magic beasts in my country, but I have heard similar stories."

"Because of that, you got everyone making a big deal about this bunch of people called adventurers."

"Adventurers—"

"Originally, they worked in sort of self-governed troupes, but now they've been systemically organized, so they're hunting more and more magical beasts. I guess farmers or the government rewards them for eliminating creatures that stray too close to crops. Adventurers are a dangerous bunch who walk around with weapons out in the open. The scale of the Adventurers' Guild has grown to the point that they've co-opted some of the rights of people to hunt and harvest crops on their own land. It seems even the kingdom's government can't quite control... Yuui?"

Ix looked at her questioningly. She was hugging herself and muttering something in a low voice. He placed a hand on her shoulder, and she leaped in response.

"What's wrong with you? You dare touch me, Yuui Laika—?"

"That's what I should be asking. Are you that hungry?" he asked.

"Oh, yes…," she answered, seemingly back to her senses. "I'm sorry—it seems I was a little out of it."

"Uh-huh. All right, what inn should we stay at?"

"I-i-inn?! At wh-what point did I say I would pay with my body?!"

"Huh?" Ix raised an eyebrow.

"…Um, I thought we were going to the wand shop?"

"There's no point. The sun's already setting. The store owner is only around during the daytime. She closes at nightfall."

Yuui blinked a few times, then nodded more strongly than he'd ever seen her before. She gripped her hood tight and spoke in a rush.

"Y-you should have said so sooner."

"I did. On the road here to Leirest. Were you so tired that you didn't hear me?"

"Uh…"

"Is that hostel over there all right with you? I'm also fine with lodging you've used before."

"I really don't mind where we stay. Oh, but I would like a private room instead of a shared one."

"A private room… I wouldn't expect a hostel to have anything like that, but I'll see what I can do."

"A-a private room for one, yes? Not a private room for two."

"Obviously. A room for two would mean you're staying with someone."

"Ah, yes…"

She pulled her hood down even farther.

2

Yuui Laika rubbed her tired eyes.

She took off her coat and threw it on the bed. The temperature was climbing in this area. Though she'd been uncomfortably hot the entire time, she wasn't bold enough to walk around outside with her face and skin exposed.

Yuui collapsed into a sitting position, unable to move further, as though her body had rooted itself there. Her legs had become stiff from the fatigue of walking nonstop since the night before.

"Agh, aaah…"

She rubbed her calf with her thumb, pain and comfort mixing perfectly until they exited from her mouth in a sigh. On top of that, her empty stomach had finally been settled with her first meal in a full day. She yawned.

Yuui wondered if she could trust that man Ix.

She knew the name Munzil. He was such a famous wand-maker that he was known even in the east, the subject of all sorts of legends that were told as if they were the truth. Tales of how his wand had allowed a child to defeat a soldier, or how he'd fixed a broken wand with a single finger, or how he'd constructed a staff from a dead branch when in distress in the forest. Obviously, those stories were quite exaggerated, but she was well aware of how amazing the products of his craftsmanship were. Solely focused on high precision, Munzil cut away everything unnecessary in a wand to the point of obsession. The wand of his she had was so natural, fit her hand so perfectly, that she hadn't understood its brilliance at first. When she happened to use one he hadn't made, she mistook it as broken because of the stark difference in performance between the two. That was when she fully understood.

But how much could she trust that apprentice of his, in terms of both his skill and his personality? He was a suspicious character. His unchanging, emotionless expression and his colorless, washed-out hair looked utterly alien to her.

There was a knock on the door.

She bolted up and replied, "Who is it?"

"It's Ix. I'm coming in."

"What?"

Before she could say anything else, Ix opened the door and peered into the room. She'd forgotten to lock the door.

"Aaaaaaah, wh-wh-what are you—?"

Yuui quickly grabbed her coat. She didn't have time to put it on properly, so she just wrapped it around her body. After doing that, however, she remembered that Ix already knew who she was. There was no reason for her to hide from him. Now that she thought about it, she realized he hadn't really reacted at all when he'd learned she was from the east.

Ix shot a glance toward her, then came into the room. He was carrying a rectangular box. It was long, thin, and wooden, with a metal handle on top. The container was large enough that it would have just barely fit into his bag. Yuui wondered if that was the only thing in his luggage.

He sat on the floor in the middle of the room. Something clanked within the box.

Yuui was confused. This didn't seem like a normal nighttime tryst at all. Her grandmother had taught her what it meant for a man to come to a woman's bedroom at night, but perhaps things were different in the kingdom.

Poking only her face out from her coat, she scolded, "What were you thinking, setting foot in a maiden's bedchamber at this hour?!"

"I was thinking I could look at the wand."

"Moreover, entering without waiting for a response is ru— The wand?"

"I have to repair it, don't I? I'll do a more detailed examination tomorrow, but I want to get a quick look now. Things will go faster that way."

"Wh-what...?"

"If you're tired, I can go."

"I—I am not tired."

"All right."

Ix nodded and opened his box, then withdrew some strange tools and spread them out on the floor. Brief preparations complete, he wrapped something around his head. When he looked up, Yuui saw he had some device over his left eye, like the opposite of a telescope. Finally, he put on a pair of white gloves.

The series of motions had been smooth and elegant, like a sword dance from a skilled warrior.

"Mm." Ix wordlessly extended his hand.

"...?"

"The wand."

"Oh, r-right."

Yuui's face flushed as she realized how fascinated she'd been. She'd felt as if he was asking her to dance.

Before he took the wand from her, he raised his arms high, then opened his hands to show their fronts and backs to her. After that, he delicately accepted the wand as if it was precious.

Among Ix's tools was an instrument that looked like a thin needle mounted on a wooden base. With careful motions, he placed the wand on the needle. It wobbled for a moment, then finally came to rest perfectly parallel to the floor. As he pushed the tip of the wand with his finger, it began to spin.

Ix scrutinized the rotating item with an expression of utter seriousness. Yuui watched from the bed, but eventually, she shyly asked a question. Otherwise, she was likely to give in to slumber.

"What was that before, that ritual?"

"Ritual?" replied Ix, adjusting the device over his left eye.

"You raised your arms and did something."

©Enji

"Oh, it's what you do before touching a wand. An...oath? Or a declaration? I'm not sure what you'd call it, but it's something like that."

"Does it mean anything?"

"It means that the wand takes priority over my life the moment I start working on it. That if there's anything the client is dissatisfied with, they have permission to cut off my arms."

"Hmm, I had no idea there were such traditions."

"Not 'were.' People still do it," corrected Ix, his gaze not moving in the slightest.

"What?"

"I have no issue with losing my arms if someone has complaints about my work. That's well within the customer's rights. And if on the off chance I break the wand, I would pay for it with my life."

There was no hint of a joke or lie in his eyes as he spoke.

"Are you serious?"

"I am."

"...Do you want to die?"

"I have no desire to lose my life. But a wand is a magic user's third arm. My master taught me to be prepared for the risks when I handle another person's arm. I'm going to polish it now."

"Huh, polish?"

Ignoring Yuui's confusion, Ix produced a dry cloth and gently rubbed the wand. Then he took out a bottle of solution to remove grime from its surface. He took off the lid, and out came a thick, white, ointment-like substance. Next, he pulled out another cloth from the box and dabbed a tiny amount of the gel on it. When he'd finished using the new cloth to polish it, the wand was beautiful beyond recognition. With the black grime that had built up from handling removed, the wand's original wood was now plain as day.

"...Now that I think about it," noted Yuui suddenly, "isn't

it a crime to repair a wand if you aren't registered with the Guild?"

"This doesn't count as repairs. Cleaning falls well within the scope of everyday maintenance."

"O-oh..." Yuui hung her head as if she'd been reprimanded.

The candlelight flickered over Ix's face. She'd known him for only a single day, but his expressionless face couldn't have prepared her for how absolutely serious he now looked. It seemed he truly did put his work above his own life.

Yuui decided that perhaps she could trust him—as a wand-maker at least.

...*That face—he looks so intense*, she thought.

The tension in his features made it abundantly clear that he would place his life on the line if need be.

And something in that expression looked very familiar...

Suddenly, that face was staring at her. "The core?"

"Wh-what?" stuttered Yuui, working her sleep-addled brain. She brought a hand to her mouth. He'd probably seen her drooling.

"Do you know what this wand's core is?" asked Ix, holding it for her to see.

The core was a material embedded in a wand that determined its characteristics. There was an infinite variety of core materials, including bones and fangs from magic beasts, stones, and plants; even human body parts were used on occasion. The greater the compatibility between the user and the core, the more they could draw out their tool's power. You might say it was the wand's heart.

The core of Yuui's wand was a red gemstone, a special material that felt slightly warm to the touch.

But there was a tiny crack in that stone.

There had been an awful shattering noise when she'd tried to cast a particular spell, and the stone had cracked. It could still be used for magic while damaged, but its power was severely reduced. Instead of releasing flames, for instance, it might instead produce sparks that wouldn't even be able to burn through the skin of your finger.

"I already know it's made from nueb wood, and I've mostly figured out how it was created. But the most important thing is the core, and that's...strange," said Ix.

"Is it a material you don't recognize?"

"Well..." Ix looked at a loss for words for a moment. "It's most likely shinee aletts, but..."

Shinee aletts, commonly known as red saintstone, was a gemstone famous for its use as a high-end core material. Ix had told Yuui it was an excellent core to have in a wand of this caliber.

"Then what are you concerned about?" she asked.

"If that's the core, then something seems a bit off to me. I mean, obviously from a cost perspective, you could say they spared no expense, but...it's not something my master would have chosen. And..."

"And?"

"No, it's just...the disposition..."

"Your roundabout way of getting to the point is making me anxious. Please just say it."

"...It's extreme. It's an incredibly moral wand."

Munzil's wands were characterized by an incredibly strong disposition; they chose their user. If wand and wielder had good compatibility, the user could gain great power. On the other hand, if they weren't compatible, and the wielder tried to use it for something against the wand's disposition, they wouldn't be able to draw out even half of its strength. That was why the slogan of Munzil's shop had been "Putting wands in the right hands."

Even Ix, who was used to seeing wands like that, thought this one was abnormal. With a mixture of admiration and frustration, he muttered, "He really went all out on this one."

Turning to Yuui, he continued. "This wand is totally abnormal, even for something my master made. That aside, I'm curious about how the shinee aletts was fabricated. I wonder what would happen if a magic user with poor compatibility tried using this thing..."

"They wouldn't be able to cast spells?"

"Maybe something even worse."

"Is it possible the core could be made from something other than shinee aletts?"

"Hmm...," muttered Ix, opening his hand. "I can think of one thing, but that can't... Well, either way, it's best to ask someone who knows. Got any ideas about the core?"

"No...I don't," replied Yuui, shaking her head.

"You don't? The wandmaker should definitely have explained that when you picked it up. Especially with my teacher. He'd talk for ages until the customer had memorized everything."

What good would that do? Yuui wondered, then said, "It was my father who ordered this wand."

"Then you should ask your father. Where is he?"

"Nowhere," she said with a sigh. "He passed away. The only things I have left to remember him by are that wand and the contract."

"I see." Ix nodded, expressionless. "Nothing we can do about that. Let's hope we can figure out what it is tomorrow with the equipment at the shop."

"Ah...okay."

Giving up on his investigations into the core material, Ix pulled out another strange tool. Yuui tried asking what he was doing just to see if he would answer. Surprisingly, he explained it all to her.

There were parts she didn't understand, but it seemed he was conducting some sort of in-depth inspection of the wand's condition. Whether its components had sustained minor damage, if it was warped, if it was degrading—all information that would be useful for its repair. Yuui had a lot to learn about wand maintenance tools, even the ones she used regularly, so soon she found herself completely absorbed in asking him question after question.

"I want to look at it a bit more, but you seem tired," noted Ix.

"I'm not...tired."

Though her eyelids had been drooping for a while now, Yuui still insisted she wasn't tired. It seemed as if her mouth couldn't keep up with what she wanted to say.

"Sure," said Ix sarcastically before dexterously gathering all the tools he'd laid out and standing. He heaved up the box by the handle, then walked to the door.

"You're going already...?" asked Yuui.

"I'm tired, too."

"Wait... There was something I wanted to ask..."

Ix stopped and turned to her.

"What is it?"

"You're not going to use test magic?"

"No." He gave a quick shake of his head.

"Why not?"

Test magic was used to determine the condition of a wand. You channeled a small amount of it into a magic catalyst to get a feel for it. It wasn't just for repairs, though; magic users also employed it in place of warm-up exercises.

"Because I can't use magic."

"...Huh?"

I must be really tired, thought Yuui dimly.

Surely she had misheard him.

What had he just said?

"Oh, and," Ix continued in his deep voice, "sorry about barging in here earlier. Next time I'll knock and wait for a response. My teacher never bothered with manners, so...sorry."

She heard the door shut, followed by footsteps.

Her eyes closed.

Yes, I must have misheard.

Yuui sank into the warmth of her bed and smiled.

Ix? Apologizing?

That rude, inconsiderate man?

No way, not possible…

3

The next day.

Yuui looked around while closely following behind Ix. As always, her hood was pulled down low, so she could see only his back. The street was jam-packed with pedestrians. She could get lost if she wasn't careful. *I've got no other choice*, she thought.

However…

"Um, is this really right?" asked Yuui.

"Is what right?" replied Ix.

"Is there really a shop around here?"

"That's why we're going this way."

"No, that's not what I meant…"

They were wandering through an older part of town, far from the city center, in an area where only lower-class people lived. The rows of buildings they'd passed consisted mostly of houses, with the occasional shop here or there. Even then, those shops were primarily bars and general-goods stores.

Wands were high-end items. Since they required valuable materials to craft and wandmakers were scarce, they always ended up being quite expensive. Even if that weren't the case, you could cast spells well only if you had received a high-level education. Plus, the kingdom didn't exactly encourage people to have wands, since they could serve as powerful weapons. Most citizens rarely encountered magic in their daily lives anyway. In fact, it seemed so dangerous that some were even averse to magic. That was why the only sorts looking to purchase a wand were a small portion of adventurers, researchers, soldiers, nobles, and students studying magic. It was a product for the rich, in other words. The average citizen had nothing to do with them.

For that reason, wand shops were typically situated in high-class areas. Their interiors were often so resplendent, they resembled a noble's manor, with trained staff who waited hand and foot on potential buyers. When Yuui had been looking for a wand shop before, she'd searched the district where the wealthy lived. Even though she hadn't brought any money, they'd all treated her respectfully. They'd even told her the location of Munzil's shop, though it was already gone by that time. Apparently, news of his death hadn't even spread to his fellow wandmakers.

But a wand shop was the last place you would think to find in the area they were in now. It seemed as if you were almost asking to get robbed if you tried to sell wands or other items here.

Sensing Yuui's anxiety, Ix said, "The land here's cheap. She didn't need much to set up shop. And she doesn't get many customers. Even though our master's name is famous, only people in the know are aware of his apprentices."

"Isn't it a problem to not get many clients?"

"It's actually a good thing. She lets her incredible skills do the talking. That way, she makes plenty from existing customers."

"When you say she's incredibly skilled, what exactly does that mean?"

"It means she's the best of all us apprentices," asserted Ix, as if it was a simple fact. "And being the best apprentice of our master means she's the best in the kingdom."

"I—I see."

"I guess you could say she's a genius... Even though she was his second-to-last apprentice, she learned her craft incredibly fast. She surpassed the others before they knew what hit them."

Yuui was behind Ix, so she couldn't see his face, but she sensed a hint of admiration in his voice. That confused her.

"If she was the second to last, that means she was before you?"

"Yep. She was the only one I lived with. The other apprentices had already moved out by the time I came along."

"Huh...," said Yuui, thinking about how horrible it would be if this other apprentice turned out to be as unfriendly as Ix. "What is her name?"

"Morna Velle."

They wound their way through the city lit by the morning sun until they came upon a stagnant water channel, where they crossed a wooden bridge that looked about to break. A horrible stench floated up from the water and made Yuui nauseated.

They continued along the channel until the road curved part-way through. Out of the row of shacks, they spied a house that appeared to be of slightly superior make. That being said, it still looked more suited for animals than people.

"......"

Yuui stared at the building, taken aback. A sign over the entrance read MORNA'S WANDS. That was the only evidence this was a place of business.

"Ah, w-wait for me," said Yuui, following Ix into the shop.

Suddenly, the smell of mold assailed her nostrils, and she couldn't help covering her nose with her coat. She frowned as she looked around the room. It took some time for her eyes to adjust to the dimness.

When she could finally see clearly, she realized the inside of the shop was just as bad as the outside. No, even worse.

The first thing that caught her attention was the large number of logs. Timber of all colors was stacked against the walls, which prevented light from coming in, leaving the room dark despite it being morning. Light from a candle wavered in the center of the room, but it was so weak, it was almost pointless.

Yuui quietly headed deeper into the store. Something strange was piled up in the corner. She moved closer. Squinting, she realized they were the corpses of magic beasts.

"Urgh..."

She quickly turned away.

It was a mountain of magic beast carcasses of all sorts of shapes and sizes. Their cloudy eyes glared at her. They must have been enchanted with a spell to prevent decay, but it wasn't a pretty sight, regardless.

Yuui realized there were magic wands and staffs lined up neatly farther into the shop, the only place properly cleaned and organized. Each of the wands and staffs was displayed with care.

Her eyes settled on one staff in particular. It was painted completely white, with a blue gem sparkling from the top. She'd never seen such a beautiful staff. It wouldn't feel out of place in the hands of a saint. Its splendor contrasted violently with the filthy shack housing it.

This place was far shabbier, messier, and stranger than any wand shop she'd ever visited.

I think this is less that wandmakers in general are weird and more that...

She glanced sideways at Ix. He seemed to have forgotten why they'd come there and was glued to one of the logs lined along the wall. She sighed.

Were all Munzil's apprentices like this? If they were, then how strange was the master himself...?

"Engraved number: 0070, Halted," came a voice by her ear out of nowhere.

"Aaah?!" Yuui shrieked, leaping back.

At some point, a boy had crept up next to her. He must have been around ten years old. The boy was short, with swaying blond hair and a small smile on his face.

"It uses good-quality artey. Its core is brilliant rosestone. It's pure but has an affinity for difficult people," continued the boy.

"U-um..."

"Though the wand's durability is excellent, it has some minor issues with tenacity. Overall evaluation is excellent. It has already been sold."

Even as she tried to interrupt the boy, he just kept staring at her and moving his mouth as if he couldn't hear her at all, the smile never leaving his face.

"Oh, Ottou. We just barged in," someone said from off to the side as the boy's spiel ceased.

Ix headed over with a hand raised in greeting. In response, the boy he called Ottou turned to him, stood stock-still for a second, then murmured, "Ix." The smile glued to his face didn't waver.

"You really helped me out with sorting through the stuff Master left behind," said Ix. "Sorry for coming to the shop all of a sudden."

"Sorting. I also received something."

"Yeah, thanks for caring," added Ix in high spirits. *Why doesn't he show that attitude toward his customers?* Yuui wondered with dissatisfaction.

"Ottou, let me introduce you," said Ix as Yuui realized his arms were spread. "This is my client. Her name is Yuui. She came to ask me to fix a wand."

The boy looked at her after blinking a few times.

"H-hello, I'm Yuui," she said, bowing her head.

"I'm Ottou."

"N-nice to meet you, Ottou."

"She's not a client," remarked the boy.

"Huh?" Yuui was confused. "What do you—?"

"True," Ix said, cutting her off.

"Can't right now," replied Ottou.

"I'm going to."

"All right."

Yuui was baffled. She looked to Ix for help, since he seemed able to have a conversation with the boy, but he refused to interpret.

"Ummm, is he...Ms. Morna's apprentice?" asked Yuui.

"No, he's just a kid from the neighborhood who comes to help her out," explained Ix. "At first, he just showed up out of curiosity, but now he handles everything outside of wand crafting. He deals with the customers, does the accounting, all that extraneous stuff."

"He looks like just a kid."

"You're probably older than he is. But when it comes to brains, he'd probably have anyone in this town beat."

"His brains?"

"He's a genius. So smart that it's scary. Honestly, if it weren't for Ottou, this shop would have collapsed by now."

"Um, I do not mean to be rude, but I find that hard to believe," admitted Yuui. "I could not understand a word he was saying."

"It's 'cause he doesn't have time for useless things like courtesy or proper sentences. Only geniuses are like that," came Ix's cheerful response. "If you don't believe me, then, hmm... Oh, if you don't mind, try taking off that hood of yours. He'll tell you something interesting."

"But..."

"Do you see anyone here who'll speak ill of you?"

Yuui glanced around to check. After confirming it was only the three of them in the shop, she removed her hood so that her characteristic skin and hair were visible.

The boy looked her way, still smiling, and froze for a few seconds.

"Ottou. What about Yuui?" asked Ix, concealing his mouth with a hand.

"Shipukk, Taakdue, Masakak, Nadam," chanted Ottou as if he was singing.

Yuui gasped. He'd just recited the names of cities near her hometown. She hadn't even told Ix that. How could Ottou have...?

But that wasn't the end of what he had to say.

"Her earring has a similar character to items belonging to the Habi royal family. Rough areas in the metalwork. A village in that city cluster has similar things. That's all."

"H-how...?"

Yuui unconsciously touched her earlobe and felt cool metal. It was true that her earring was proof of her bloodline, but no one in the kingdom should have been able to recognize its significance.

Pulling her hood back up, she asked Ix to explain.

"Apparently, he does this by comparing what's in front of him with what's in his memory," he said.

"What does that mean?"

"You might meet someone similar to someone else or see an object that resembles something else you've encountered. You do it, too, yeah?"

"Yes, but..."

"I told you. Ottou's a genius," insisted Ix, spreading his hands with his palms up. "His memory and observational skills are way above average. He can tell your place of origin, your tribe, and even your family relations just by looking at your facial features or bone structure. The kid can also intuit your position and social standing based on your clothes and mannerisms. Guess he's always been like that. 'Cause there are people of all social classes from inside and outside the kingdom gathering in this city. That makes him perfectly suited for gathering information. With those skills, he—"

"Are you saying he can tell I'm one of the minority Lukutta people?"

Lukutta was a country to the east. The kingdom invaded it several years ago. Though they fought back for all they were worth, they had to surrender their ravaged land in the end. According to the kingdom, Lukutta was their "eastern ally." In reality, however, the kingdom had forced Lukutta to give up its people, land, and resources, so the region was now nothing more than a powerless vassal state.

The sun shifted; a thin ray of light poured into the shop.

Something clinked. Yuui looked over to find Ottou arranging

the wands and staffs. He moved lackadaisically, making tiny adjustments to each wand's location. The boy seemed to have lost all interest in Yuui. Actually, it would be more accurate to say he hadn't had any interest in her in the first place. He'd simply pointed out that certain things resembled other things.

She felt somehow discouraged and let out a sigh.

Ix shrugged and urged her to follow before opening a door leading into a room in the back of the shop.

"Well, that's Ottou for you. He's a good kid. Not many people understand him, since he's so out there. Apparently, he gets treated like a nuisance at home, too, but still, he's a good kid," said Ix quickly, as though he was making an excuse.

"It's all right. I understand he didn't have any ill intentions," said Yuui.

"And, uh..." Ix's expression was changing so quickly, it made Yuui wonder what had happened to his normal unsociability. She smiled awkwardly as he said, "So what I'm trying to say is..."

"Yes?"

"Morna's so specialized in making wands that she needs a genius like Ottou. So, uh, you remember how I said you can only meet her during the daytime?"

"I do."

"What that really meant is, Ottou's only in the shop then."

4

They made their way to what looked like a storage room. It was surprisingly organized, with slender objects neatly lining the shelves. As soon as they entered, they saw a door leading to the garden to their left. No one was there right now. Brilliant white light poured in from a small window at the end of the storage room. Near it was another door on the left-hand side. It appeared this property consisted solely of the shop, the storage room, the middle garden, and a rear room.

Yuui watched Ix knock on the door.

"Morna, it's Ix."

There was no reply.

He looked at Yuui. After exchanging nods, he placed his hand on the door.

As the door scraped open, they heard the sound of a few objects thumping to the floor.

Ix paid that no mind and walked in.

"Sorry to disturb you," said Yuui quietly as she followed behind him. However—

"Huh? Huh?"

She couldn't find anywhere to put her foot down, so she ended up wavering with one leg in the air as the room came into view.

Wooden boxes and paper bundles were heaped on either side of the door. One of those mountains seemed to have collapsed in an avalanche, and it was spread all over the floor. Something like black cloth was also draped over the floor. On closer inspection, she realized it was clothing.

Yuui stepped back out into the storage room for a moment to get a view of the entire rear room. She let out a sigh, lost for words.

She'd thought the mess in the shop was bad, but that was nothing compared with the catastrophe in here.

The floorboards were entirely invisible, obscured by a chaotic mix of everyday items, clothing, several strange tools, wood (of course), magic beast corpses, other things that appeared to be materials, and what looked like dirty garbage.

The only place in the room you could even think of calling tidy was the area around the workstation in the back. The chair was free of any clutter, and only a few wands in progress and a knife for working on them rested on top of the desk. Similar tools were scattered over the floor nearby.

Ignoring this disaster of a room, Ix casually stepped on the items strewn across the floor until he was near the middle of it all.

Then he leaned over and reached a hand into a small mountain of rags near the work desk. Since piles of trash were blocking her view, Yuui couldn't see what was there.

The pile swallowed Ix's arm as he touched it. When his arm was concealed up to the elbow, it gave a violent tremor.

"There we go—fished her out," he announced, pulling back his hand. The trash and cloth fell to the ground to reveal a human being.

"Yikes!" cried Yuui as she recoiled. The light of the sun allowed her to get a clear look at the person's condition.

It was a woman with long hair.

Her disheveled locks fell to her waist, with flyaways going in every direction. She wore a giant smock with a hole for her head to come through that appeared to have been resewn on numerous occasions. The cloth was untreated but dark, and it seemed too small on her. Actually, it looked ridiculous, tight around the chest, then falling limply down from there. Even so, it obviously wasn't long enough, as Yuui could see part of the woman's bare leg peeking out near the floor. Her ankles were thin, like twigs. They seemed ready to snap.

She was tall, perhaps nearly as tall as Ix, but her poor posture made her seem shorter. Her eyes were half open and lacked any sort of life. There was a trace of drool on her chin.

"Uhhh....," groaned the woman quietly.

Either she'd just been roused, or she was still half asleep. She pulled on Ix's arm and rubbed it hard across her face. Was she trying to clean it off? There must have been some paint or varnish on her face because his sleeve cuff turned black. Yuui didn't miss the slight frown on his expressionless visage.

I see, she thought.

Yuui had only these two to go off, but she was starting to understand what sort of people Munzil had taken on as apprentices.

"Wake up," demanded Ix.

"Aaaaaaah…agh." Though the woman remained in place for a little while after Ix waved his arm, she crumpled to the ground before long.

The woman sat up, touching the back of her head where she'd struck it hard. "Ow…" She rubbed her eyes and looked around. "…wie?"

"Morning, Morna," greeted Ix flatly.

"I-Ixie."

Ixie? thought Yuui, feeling faint.

The woman, Morna, spent a few seconds with her mouth agape. But when she looked at Ix's face, she started making a *fee, fyuu* sound that was neither breathing nor speech. Her mouth was oddly twisted.

"I—I—I…," she stammered.

"Last night, I told you I'd come over once I got everything sorted," reminded Ix.

"R-really? Fee, fyuu…"

"You forgot. I figured you might."

"Hee, hee-hee-hee…" Morna let out a disconcerting sound as her shoulders shook.

Yuui realized that the strange sound Morna had been making was her way of laughing. It wasn't that she lacked the energy to use her voice or that she was groggy from being woken up; that was just how she was.

Morna rose unsteadily to her feet. Her neck flopped like a baby's as she looked around the room. Then her gaze fell on the door. Her eyes met Yuui's.

Suddenly, Morna grew pale. She retreated a few steps, mouth half open, before backing into the wall and letting out a groan.

©Enji

"I-Ixie, th-th-th-th-that girl…"

Morna trembled, looking terrified. This went far beyond shyness of strangers. The extent of her fear actually made Yuui feel guilty.

"Oh, you don't have to worry about her," Ix told Yuui as he saw her attempt to exit the room. "Morna's always like this with people she meets for the first time. She'll get better if you spend some time together."

"U-uh-huh…"

"H-hey, Ixie, don't i-ignore me…," cried Morna, tears welling up in her eyes as she clung to Ix's sleeve.

"This is one of Master's customers. He's dead, so she came to me," explained Ix simply. "It's a wand repair and maintenance job. I want you to lend me some tools and your assistance."

"A c-customer?"

"That's right. She has a contract from Master."

Both of them turned to look at Yuui, who stepped forward and bowed her head.

"My name is Yuui. I apologize for any inconvenience we have caused, Ms. Morna."

"Yuui…," mumbled Morna.

"Yes."

"……"

Morna stared at her with damp eyes. Yuui thought they looked like translucent emeralds. They stared at each other for a few seconds. After a moment of silence, Morna violently broke eye contact.

"U-uh, um… T-t-tea…," she gasped.

"No thank you, I'm all right," replied Yuui.

"Wh-wh-where was…?"

"Calm down, I'll get it," reassured Ix.

He deftly placed his right hand on Morna's head as it swiveled left and right. He kept holding on to her back until she let out a "feeyuu" and stopped moving.

She plopped into the chair and looked up at Ix with puppy-dog eyes.

"Th-thank you," she said.

"Mm."

"Oh, I'll prepare the tea. If you don't mind telling me where I should go?" said Yuui.

She almost sprinted out of the room. Yuui definitely didn't have the courage yet to be alone with Morna.

5

With the new face gone, Morna managed to achieve a semblance of calm. She looked here and there around the busy room, her fingers squirming like a millipede's legs, but that was normal for her.

Ix gazed at Morna, which made her cringe with fear. She looked up hesitantly.

"Oh, s-sorry," she managed.

"For what?"

"Uh, w-well, nothing really..."

"All right."

"Yeah."

"......"

"Oh..."

She opened and closed her mouth, making noises that could have been words or something else entirely. Though she wasn't good at talking with people, she also couldn't stand silence. It was a nasty combination of personality quirks.

"Oh, r-r-right," she said tensely. "Show me."

"Show you what?"

"Uh, the c-contract. You h-have it, right?"

Morna was like their master in that she had excellent

wandmaking skills but horrific interpersonal skills. In fact, she was probably worse than their master. At least Munzil had managed his own shop. And in some ways, she was his exact opposite, since he was always very aggressive toward everyone, whereas she was always afraid.

After passing her eyes over the letter, Morna placed it carefully on her work desk.

"I—I see…"

"Seriously, he's left us an incredibly inconvenient contract. And I thought I'd just finished sorting out everything he'd left behind." Ix sighed.

"W-well, we should still repair it…right?"

"Yeah. The core's broken, though."

As he explained that he couldn't figure out what material was in the core, Morna seemed perplexed.

"Y-you mean, even you couldn't figure it out?"

"There's only so much investigation I could do. I don't have magic anyway."

"I suppose so…," said Morna, lifting the contract. "A-all right, I'll take on this job."

"Huh?"

"What?"

They looked at each other questioningly.

"Uh, w-well, I…," whined Morna.

"No, I'm not angry," said Ix, raising one hand placatingly as Morna trembled, tears in her eyes. "It's not that. I was just asking why you'd take the job. It says right there, doesn't it? In a way, I'm the 'simpleton who read it first'…"

"B-b-but…" Morna stopped herself there before continuing. "I-it says 'c-craftsman'?"

"Oh…" Ix heaved a dull sigh, unable to prevent the sound from escaping his lips.

She was correct. The contract did indeed say "a craftsman who apprenticed under Munzil." Of course it would.

The thing was, Ix wasn't a craftsman.

It was exactly as he'd told Yuui.

That meant the wand's repair would fall to Morna, so it would have nothing to do with him anymore. Her skills were significantly better than his anyway, and someone without leeway in his coin purse wasn't in a position to take on a free job. Realistically, it was also the better option for the client.

However—

"No, I can't put this burden on you, Morna." His mouth moved before it had time to catch up with his thoughts.

"Huh? B-but—"

"I'll do the repair. I just have to register with the Guild, right?"

"You sure?"

"Yeah. Unlike you, I don't have any other work lined up anyway. You just need to help me in the beginning."

"Mm..." Morna nodded, albeit uneasily.

"I get why you're worried," Ix replied with a snort, "but even someone as unskilled as me can handle swapping a core out."

"Ah, no, your capability isn't the problem..."

"Oh, funding? Luckily, I've got some cash saved up for now, so I'm fine."

"Mmmm, money isn't, well, um, that's also a problem, true, but that wasn't what I meant...," she said, shaking her head slightly. "Wh-wh-why are you doing it?"

"I told you; it'd be a burden for—"

"I-it's not really that big of a deal. It's Master's wand. I w-want to check it out, too."

"Ah..." Ix frowned. "Well, that's fine, I guess. But you can leave it to me. It's my first job after all."

"R-really? First job... Hee-hee..."

He didn't get what was so funny, but it appeared he'd convinced Morna with that, because she didn't question him further.

So...why am I? he asked himself.

It being his first assignment wasn't a good enough reason.

Not only would he be better off if he left it to Morna, but also it was something he should leave to her anyway. In other words, he was being selfish.

Was he really taking up this annoying job his master left him out of selfishness?

He didn't understand his own decision.

A crease sat between his eyebrows for a while, but eventually, he sighed and decided to forget the question. The breath he let out stirred the dust in the air. It spread and disappeared.

6

Yuui prepared the tea in scattered vessels, then returned to the room.

Morna slurped the tea, her fear of Yuui fading slightly. Even so, Morna refused to make eye contact with her, instead staring at her feet as she spoke.

"S-so the, uh, wand…"

"Thank you for examining it," said Yuui.

"Fuu, heh-heh-heh…"

Morna accepted the wand, recoiling from Yuui as she did so. Cradling it in both hands, she gently transferred it to the work desk. Then she performed the same ritual Ix had.

In contrast with Ix's polished motions, Morna's were disconcerting. She slouched even worse and stared at the wand creepily while she inspected it. As she swayed her body to and fro, she occasionally let out a giggle.

"All right," Ix murmured quietly, bringing his face close to her ear. "It was made in the year… Its transmission efficiency is… The adoption method was a type-two Rednoff pipe transfer… Its disposition is incredibly moral… Estimated flexion rate is…"

Yuui wondered vaguely if the hair scratching his face didn't bother him.

For nearly an hour, Morna used complex instruments to investigate the wand. Ix stood next to her, lending a hand. Surely their inspection would be finished soon.

But their expressions weren't promising. Deep furrows lined their brows, and their faces were beset with confusion. They'd just removed the wand from an instrument that had a large crystal set in its middle.

"You agree, right?" murmured Ix. "The cycle is strange for a shinee aletts core."

"The R-R-Rednoff type could explain it," Morna replied, shaking her head. "It speeds up the junction..."

"With extreme affinity?"

"Y-yeah."

"Well, it's an interesting thought from a theoretical standpoint, but not even Master could ensure that kind of precision. Besides, it wouldn't function as a wand."

"Oh yeah..." Morna swiveled her head. She was so completely engrossed in the world of wands that she didn't even react when she turned toward Yuui.

"I have to try using it...," said Morna.

"Will that be okay?" asked Ix.

"Y-yeah. Probably. It'll work."

"All right." Ix nodded, walked over to Yuui, then leaned against the wall next to her and crossed his arms. He watched over Morna with an intense expression.

"Excuse me, what is she doing...?" asked Yuui.

"Test magic. Stay back—it's dangerous," replied Ix.

"Dangerous?"

"It's been a while since she's used that instrument, and she isn't exactly a great spellcaster. It might explode."

Before Yuui could ask in more detail, Morna announced, "H-h-here I go."

She remounted the wand in the instrument they were using before and closed her eyes. Yuui knew this part well. People who weren't used to using magic often focused like that.

Morna drew in a long breath and cast the spell.

Test magic didn't create light or sound, so Yuui felt only the flow of mana. The volume and quantity Morna produced were both fairly decent. You could say she had plenty of potential as a magic user, but her handling was rough. It was obvious she hadn't been trained in it.

After maintaining the spell for a few seconds, Morna let out a sigh.

"I'm done," she said, looking over at them.

"Yeah?" Ix tucked his chin in slightly. "So?"

"Mm, mm..." Morna glanced at the instrument, and her mouth curled with a "fuuee."

"Morna?" asked Ix.

"Foo-fyu-fyuu-fyuu..."

"Wh-what's wrong, Ms. Morna?!" asked Yuui, but she didn't reply. Instead, she swayed her shoulders as drool dripped from her mouth.

Yuui glanced up at Ix's face. He looked shocked, but that expression slowly brightened until he let out a cry of delight in the end.

"No way!" he shouted.

"Hee, way...," said Morna.

"Ha-ha-ha! I can't believe Master's bullshit story was true. Makes sense..."

"I'll h-have to investigate more. It m-might be reusable if I reshape it..."

"Hold up, wait. That's my customer's wand. First I..."

The two gathered around the wand, creepy smiles on their faces.

Yuui timidly asked, "Pardon my interruption, but what are the two of you so happy about?"

"Oh yeah, Yuui," replied Ix, his face betraying that he'd just remembered her existence. "Long story short, we know what the core material is."

"It isn't shinee aletts?"

"No. It's actually something completely different. I'd thought it might be a possibility, but I can't believe I was right."

"So…what is it?"

"Well…don't be surprised when you hear."

"Please just get to the point already," Yuui said with an exasperated sigh. "It is my wand after all."

"It's dragon heart."

"What?" Yuui blinked a few times, unable to believe her own ears.

"It's dragon. Dragon heart," said Ix, deeply impressed. "I thought our master was just bullshitting us when he said he'd made a wand with dragon heart before. But I've got no choice but to believe it when the real thing is right in front of me."

"Dragon…?"

"Yep. No doubt about it, right, Morna?"

She nodded emphatically. "Th-th-that's the only possibility. It's absolutely dragon heart. There's nothing else it could be."

"Huh…" Yuui was confused. "And that's what the two of you are happy about?"

"Of course," said Ix. "Why aren't you? What's with that strange reaction? This is an amazing wand. Who was your dad?"

"No, what I want to know is, is this material easy to get?" asked Yuui.

"Of course not," replied Ix immediately. "Morna and I didn't even believe it until now, and we heard the story straight from Master's mouth. We can't even be sure any more exists other than what we have here."

"Um…then how are you planning to fix my wand?"

"Huh?" Ix stared at Morna.

She stared back wordlessly.

After a few moments of silence, the two looked at Yuui at the same time.

"Are you really telling me you two were that excited just because you got a chance to see a rare material?" she said incredulously.

If what she knew was correct, dragons had been extinct for over a thousand years.

1

Three days passed.

Yuui entered the wand shop to find only Ottou, the shop manager. He was taking logs out of the stacks one by one and tapping them with a wooden mallet to check how they sounded. Apparently, it was to see how they were drying. He cast spells on them with a variety of wands, both to check their functionality and to produce new materials at the same time.

Ottou didn't react to the sound of the door opening and instead continued working, completely absorbed in his task.

"I'm back...," said Yuui quietly as she placed a basket down. Inside were several oddly thick bones—the spine of a magic beast she'd been asked to purchase.

Apparently, a merchant would swing by every few days and take Morna's order. When it came to wandmaking materials, she was such a good customer that the merchant would personally travel all the way to her shop to deliver the goods despite the fact that the trip ate into their profits. That was what led to the mountain of corpses in the corner of the room. They could carve up the carcasses whenever they needed something, and each part had its own use.

But this was a special instance of core repair. Morna needed specific parts from magical beasts she didn't often use. Yuui had offered to purchase them directly, since it was faster that way. She'd spent the last three days schlepping back and forth between the city and the shop.

Ix had told her he couldn't make a client help, but she was free to assist him of her own volition. Since Leirest was a city full of cultures from various places, she thought it might be fun to have a look around. As someone from the east, though, she thought a casual sightseeing trip was off the table.

The materials they asked her to buy were a bit icky, but she far preferred people being grossed out at her for walking around with magic beast bones over them staring at her with curiosity or scorn. No one had approached her and told her to take down her hood, at the very least.

Just as she was about to go tell Ix and Morna she'd returned, a muffled boom echoed from the back room.

"...They seem busy. Perhaps I'll wait a little while," she said to herself.

Taking a breath, Yuui sat down on a chair in the store. Explosions were an everyday occurrence in this shop. All she could do was ignore them. Once, she'd gone into Morna's room because she'd been worried something bad had happened, but that had turned out terribly.

She could hear wings flapping on the roof overhead.

There hadn't been any signs of a customer showing up. Yuui hadn't seen a single one since she'd come here. Ix had told her Morna only got clients who were aware of her skill, but at this point, Yuui was starting to wonder if even that was true.

Suddenly, she looked up to find Ottou staring at her from the center of the shop.

"Yuui Laika," he said.

"Yes, hello, Ottou."

"Your questions?"

"Hmm? Oh, about that..."

The more she spent time with him, the more she realized Ottou never bothered with unnecessary details; he just got straight to the point. In this case, he was reminding her that she'd spent the past few days asking him a variety of questions and was now inquiring if she had anything else she wished to mention today.

"Oh, that's right," said Yuui as she clasped her hands in front of her chest. "Ix said he couldn't use magic before. Is that true?"

"It is."

"But…I've never heard of a person not being able to use magic. Every single human has magic in them. There's a question about the amount and quality, of course, but anyone should be able to hold a wand and cast a spell."

"There are some instances of loss of magical ability as a symptom of sonim."

"Huh?"

Ottou spoke smoothly as he continued. "The majority of pregnant women who contract sonim die. Even if the mother survives, their child will be stillborn. There have been some very rare cases, however, where the pregnancy still goes through. Children who survive a sonim birth lack magic and are unable to cast spells. One such instance was recorded in the kingdom."

"And that was…Ix?"

"No. It was the child of a noble who died later on. Ix's parents are unknown, so we can't say for sure whether they were infected with sonim."

It made sense that there wouldn't be records of the lives and deaths of common folk, who would have never had a chance to use magic anyway.

"I see… Thank you, Ottou." Yuui nodded.

Ottou shut his mouth and returned to work. After pulling a carcass from the mountain of magic beast corpses, he went to the back garden. He was probably going to skin and treat it.

So it really was true that Ix couldn't cast spells. Yuui sighed.

He hadn't used test magic, and it had seemed as if he hadn't sensed the mana that Morna had used. No way could there be someone like that. Or so Yuui had thought...

She wondered if he would be able to hack it as a wandmaker after all. Even though it wasn't her problem, it still made her anxious. Ix wouldn't be able to adjust the wands he made himself. That was like a chef with no tongue.

Just then, there was a particularly loud explosion.

"Aah!"

Yuui cowered and looked around.

Dust fell from the ceiling as the building trembled from the shock wave. A few logs tumbled. The only objects that withstood the blast with a minimal amount of shaking were the wands and staffs, which were affixed to the shelves.

Eventually, silence returned to the room like a recoil.

The moment all was still, she heard the door open, and Ix poked his head in. He was scowling. Dark bags hung beneath his eyes; he probably hadn't slept much in the past three days. The clothes he was wearing were somewhat dirty.

He sat down on the shop floor and gave a dry cough.

"A-are you all right?" asked Yuui automatically.

"Huh? ...Oh, Yuui," he said, rubbing his eyes before finally noticing her.

"I bought the things you asked for," she said.

"Things?"

"Um, the bones...," she reminded him, lifting the basket for him to see.

"Oh, that...," he said faintly, perhaps from lack of sleep.

"You will use them, won't you?"

"No, don't need to. It didn't work."

"Hmm? What didn't work?"

"I'm out of ideas," snapped Ix. "If the results of that last experiment had been good, I would have used them, but they weren't. So I don't need them anymore."

"In other words—"

"We give up. We can't repair that core. Unfortunately."

It took Yuui a while to process his emotionless words.

Is he saying that...the wand is unfixable? she thought.

Ix saw her fighting for words and added, "Well, it's not like we got nothing out of the experiments. We did manage to come extremely close to your core's properties by synthesizing shinee aletts with agnasite, among other things. It's really interesting, from a wand craft perspective. I might call it a 'compound core.' I bet it'd spread like crazy among craftsmen if we wrote a book. Morna wouldn't be up to it, though..."

"I don't care about that," Yuui told him.

"No? I thought it was a pretty amazing idea."

Yuui cleared her throat and coughed. Wands were everything to those two. She couldn't keep up with every little detail of their obsessions.

"You got close to the properties...but that's not good enough?" asked Yuui.

"No. The compound outputs far less power than the original core. That's dragon hearts for you. They're literally in an entirely different league compared with the other core types."

"So you are saying you cannot make a perfect re-creation."

"There's one other problem, too."

"What's that?" she said with a sigh.

"This compound core technique has never been attempted before. There's no guarantee it would work."

"...Um, you were making light of it before, but you did say that if you failed and broke a wand, you would pay with your life, yes?"

"The technique should go well, in theory."

"...Right."

"Sorry I'm not good enough," said Ix weakly before letting out a big yawn. They knew the core material was from a dragon, a creature of legend, so finding a replacement was bound to be taxing. But Ix's casual attitude toward the situation left Yuui feeling torn between getting angry with him and trying to comfort him.

"Right, what do you want to do?" asked Ix.

"What can we do?"

"Swap the core with the compound core, though that only re-creates the properties of the original. Then sell off the dragon heart. A thing like that belongs in a national treasure vault, so it'd probably net you a fortune. If it fails... Well, there's no way I could make the same thing, but I'd make you the best wand I possibly could before I kicked the bucket."

"...Do you want to lose your life?"

"No." Ix's expression was serious as he shook his head. "It's not like I make wands in order to die."

In order to die...

Yuui fell silent, her face the same as that of someone else's in her mind for just a moment.

"......"

"What's wrong?" he asked.

"N-nothing," she stammered, quickly ridding her face of any emotion. "Anyway, I'd be in big trouble if you failed. I absolutely need that wand—"

"Hold on," interrupted Ix meaningfully, spreading his arms and stopping her.

He yawned again. Yuui noticed his cheeks were sunken and his features were gaunt. Perhaps he'd been so excited to examine the dragon heart that he hadn't been getting enough to eat.

"We do have one other option," he said, holding up a finger.

"Huh...? Which is?"

"We find a dragon heart."

"...Dragons no longer exist."

"We don't need a living one. We just need a heart. Actually, that's not even true. We just have to find something with the same material."

"The same material? That's a strange way of putting it."

"I just corrected what I said before to be more accurate. We've been calling it dragon heart, but we don't actually know for certain that's what it really is."

"Um, I thought Mr. Munzil said it was?"

"All Master told us was its name—'dragon heart'—its characteristics, and its properties so we could tell it apart from other substances. That's it. We have no proof your core is actually a real dragon's heart. Master said he was looking at some dragon bones at a castle when he was young and that was the only thing this material resembled, so he named it 'dragon heart.' How much of that is true, I'm not so sure. We're going with this nomenclature but only because we don't have a better idea. It's possible it's just a rare gemstone with powerful properties. In fact, a number of things about this substance resemble stone."

"And what do you think, personally?"

"Well," Ix said with a shrug, "I guess it's probably got some connection to dragons... That's about it."

"Huh?" Yuui blinked, not expecting that answer. "And what proof do you have of that?"

"Master might not have been completely on the mark, but, you know, he wasn't the type to outright lie. Even if we don't go all the way and say it's a heart."

As much as I talk poorly about the guy, I trust him, thought Ix, though he didn't vocalize it.

"Regardless of what you say about its connection to dragons, I cannot help feeling it's pointless because they are extinct," argued Yuui.

"But you can't say it's impossible. That's what I reckon anyway," countered Ix, placing a hand on the wall as he stood. "Besides, I think a few people have got to know about what this stuff is."

"Everyone has heard legends of dragons..."

"Exactly. They appear in stories from every single country.

But then if you ask someone if they think dragons actually existed, they'll say no. A legend's just a legend. There might be some people who think they probably did exist, but there's almost certainly no one who's certain. Of course not—nobody can guarantee what happened thousands of years ago. But we're different."

"Because we have the real thing..."

"Yep. Setting aside our doubts about its authenticity, there's probably no one in the world who's seriously looking for this material. Which is why we can have hope. We know for sure this substance exists, so that's half the job done right there."

"But even if we do find it, we can't be certain if we'll be able to buy it or convince someone to give it to us. Would it really be that easy to get a hold of?"

"Well, that is true. Morna and I don't have that kind of money. How about you, Yuui?"

"No." She shrugged.

"Even if we do find it, we don't know if we can get our hands on it. We also don't know how long it would take to acquire. Hell, we don't even have a single clue on where to start looking. It's possible we could spend a decade on this and it would still end in failure."

"It is quite uncertain, yes."

"So what do you want to do?" Ix asked. He looked at Yuui while rubbing his hands together as if saying, "I've laid out all the options—now it's up to the buyer to make the call."

Yuui thought for a few moments, but she didn't have to wrestle with the issue for very long.

"...Let's impose a deadline, then," she proposed.

"Okay?"

"I don't have that much time. I cannot be without my wand forever. Therefore, we shall look for the dragon material first. If we reach the deadline, we will give up and settle for the compound core. It should at least have the power of a normal wand with that, right?"

"Yes. But a high-end wand. And if that's the case, I can prepare you a replacement for you to use in the meantime, which would let us search thoroughly. This wand is powerful, but I doubt you'd have anything soon that'd make you need—"

"No, I need that wand."

"You've got something that pressing? I don't know if you're planning on going to war or what."

"O-of course it's not something as absurd as that. Um…well, it is the single memento my father left me. It feels wrong to treat it like some decoration collecting dust while I use another wand."

"…All right, I understand." Ix nodded, his expression unchanging.

He turned on his heel and headed for the back room. Yuui went with him.

Looking up at him, she asked, "You really wanted to find the dragon material, didn't you?"

"The customer's wishes take priority. That's the craftsman's code," replied Ix firmly, most likely feeling some disappointment. He seemed to mean what he said, though. Yuui frowned slightly.

She saw Ottou in the back garden, a deboning knife in his small hand. Sliced-off portions of carcass lined the surrounding area. The butchering was going well.

The door to the back room was still open.

Yuui took one step in and grimaced.

"What happened here…?"

Morna's room was in an even worse condition.

Obviously, it had been messy before, but it at least had a kind of logic to it. At minimum the magic beast parts had been with the other parts, and the tools had been with the other tools.

But now, Yuui couldn't even fathom how to describe it. Morna's dwelling seemed like the place furthest from order in the entire world.

Lacking the energy to be any more careful, she decided to give in.

As Yuui resigned herself, Ix spoke with Morna about their next steps.

"...And so I want information. You don't have any connections, do you, Morna?" he asked.

"Mm, no," Morna said, before clapping her sickly pale hands in realization. "Oh, that's right. I-Ixie, h-how about you go to the library?"

"Library? That's the place with lots of books, right?" asked Ix, confused.

"Y-yep, that's it."

"Uh-huh...I might find a book about dragons."

"Y-yeah!"

"Well, actually...," said Yuui, cocking her head while Morna and Ix were getting excited.

It seemed they didn't know much about libraries.

Yuui had heard they were becoming popular in the kingdom. Lately, influential cities throughout the regions were building one after the other. Merely having one in town was a status symbol.

However, the kingdom's book collections couldn't match the quality of the libraries it had built to house them. Apparently, many of the volumes in their large collections had holes, and the librarians pushed you to see a lot of dubious magic tomes and scraps of paper. Those were the nasty rumors going around, at least. The only quality texts in the kingdom's holdings were Marayist scriptures.

Marayism was the religion widely followed in the west. At present, the kingdom was a theocracy, and its sovereign also acted as the head of the Maray Church. When theocracy was established about a hundred years back, it swept away the indigenous religions of the region. The scattered Maray scriptures from that time ended up being housed in libraries. As a side note, while the kingdom seemed to have thought that this would increase the number of devout believers, a new order of followers had been rebelling against the state church, accusing it of acting against scripture. This was causing chaos in the kingdom.

Anyway, Yuui hadn't heard good things about the libraries, so she wasn't getting her hopes up.

"Ah, oh, but...," Morna said, suddenly biting her finger. "I heard only certain people can go in there..."

"You need a library pass," interjected Yuui. The two whipped around, and she looked away in discomfort.

"You know a lot about it?" asked Ix.

"You can apply for a pass with the head librarian, which they will issue after a screening. The head librarian position is normally filled with a retired noble, so you would be hard-pressed to say it's truly open to the general public," explained Yuui.

Ix and Morna stared at each other, an uncomfortable silence settling in the room.

"...We'll think of another way," Ix said with a sigh.

"Y-y-yeah." Morna clasped her hands and nodded. "Oh... Wh-wh-what if we ask Big Sis? B-by letter?"

"...Her? Are you serious?" asked Ix.

"Mm... Oh, that's right. There's a c-customer who placed an order wh-who knows a lot about that stuff."

"Hmm? When are they coming?"

"Soon, p-probably. Definitely."

Ix shook his head without a word, then turned to Yuui. "Oh yeah, there's something I need to ask you."

"What is it?" replied Yuui.

"You said you're putting a deadline on this. When would that be, specifically? It might affect how we search."

"I would like this done by the end of the summer."

"Summer this year?"

"Yes."

"That's soon..." Ix frowned. "So we've got to do as targeted a search as soon as we can. It's a gamble. Is there a reason you're in that much of a hurry?"

"Yes...," she started, but he looked as if he was going to question her more, so she changed the subject. "Um, about the library you were discussing earlier, would you like to accompany me there?"

"You have a pass?" asked Ix.

"Even without a pass, there is a system that allows you to use public libraries. So long as you meet certain conditions."

"Conditions?"

"Such as being a student of the Royal Academy."

"Huh?"

An expression showed on Ix's face that she'd never seen before. It was a vacant, dumbfounded look that reminded Yuui of a stupefied-looking bird that lived around her homeland.

"Meaning," said Ix, opening a hand and glancing meaningfully at her, "you're a student?"

"I am," replied Yuui, nodding as she forced her smile to stay on her face.

"And 'by the end of the summer' means..."

"I would like you to manage something during the Academy's break, Ix. I won't be able to take magic courses without my wand."

"Break?" Ix looked up and was quiet for a while. Then he opened his mouth slightly and ventured, "You sure a temporary replacement won't do?"

"What happened to that craftsman's code of yours?"

2

There were pages upon pages of yellowed paper covered in black writing. To be honest, the sight made Ix uncomfortable. Books were strange objects, and a library filled with them was beyond his comprehension. Why did those in power admire these places so much? He couldn't figure it out. Or perhaps they admired them because they didn't understand them, either...

He turned the page and sighed. He'd had high hopes for the history books, but they mostly just listed previous kings' accomplishments. There was nothing in there about dragons.

Ix's master had taught him to read. He'd told him, "I'll teach you a bit," then locked Ix in the storage room until he'd memorized all the characters. It seemed the man wasn't versed in any actual teaching methods. Munzil would shut him in there whenever he could, and Ix would study through his tears.

"I brought more... Oof."

Yuui had returned, with so many books in her arms that he couldn't see her small frame. She set them down with a thud next to the mountain of tomes already there.

The piles surrounding Ix were stacked high enough to reach his waist. He closed the volume he'd finished reading and placed it in another stack.

"I've finished these ones. Take them back," he said.

"...All right," she replied. Slumping her shoulders, she picked up that stack.

He watched her forlorn figure move away.

Ix picked up another book and swept away a silverfish crawling on it. He didn't think this title looked promising, either.

Yuui's position had allowed them to enter the library, but thus far it had gone like this, so they hadn't accomplished much of anything. First of all, the newer books didn't mention dragons at all. Yuui and Ix then turned their focus to things like fairy tales and legends, but even when the beasts were mentioned, the tomes they featured in didn't provide the information Ix wanted, like specific locations, names, and years.

Of course, that was how it should be. Dragons were legendary magic beasts, the last of which had expired long ago. Why would detailed accounts of them still remain? He'd been foolish for hoping to find information in a fairy tale.

"…Hmm?"

The character for *dragon* suddenly flew past his eyes.

But he lost hope after reading the surrounding text.

> **"Magic can enact anything one could imagine"—This hypothesis was disproved with the below argument. The volume of mana within a creature is limited by its body. Even among races such as the elves, who have specialized internal structures, there is an upper limit to the mana they can possess. It is impossible to have unlimited magic. Once this conclusion was reached, the magic research field split into two primary fields. These were standard magicology, which investigates ways to economize a person's mana, and special magicology, or the so-called "dragon magic," which presupposes an unlimited supply of mana.**

It was an introduction to magic, which, for some reason, had the word *dragon* in its explanation. That was all.

"What the hell."

Ix tapped the author's name, Shigan Aym, with his finger.

Even though this was a library, that didn't mean they had an endless number of books. It seemed he'd already moved on to tomes that weren't closely related to dragons.

It had already been quite some time since they'd started coming to the library. The research they were doing might have been foolhardy, but he was itching to get a move on.

"No luck today, either?" came a voice.

"Huh?" Ix looked up to see himself reflected back in a pair of gleaming eyes.

It was an elderly woman, or so she appeared.

On closer inspection, she looked old, but he wasn't entirely convinced that was the case. Her croaking voice, small body, and long white hair were all telltale signs of a senior citizen. Even her back was hunched with age. But those eyes that gazed at him... Those golden saucers were alive with light and sparkled with youth, as though they were the eyes of a five-year-old.

"You've been here every day. It appears you are searching quite diligently for something. Mm, there are rarely people here who read so enthusiastically," she told him. While Ix sat there, taken aback, the woman continued on in her crisp manner of speaking. "I do wish you would read a little more thoroughly, though. You skim so carelessly that I feel bad for the books."

Ix watched for a break in her speech so he could ask who she was, and her eyes shone again.

"Oh, you would like to know who I am? I am the head librarian. Aren't libraries just wonderful?"

"...Yeah," he managed, staring hard at her.

There was always a middle-aged man at the entrance, so Ix had assumed he was the one in charge. He'd thought that someone who'd lost their place as head of the family to another relative had taken up the position in this city, rather than a retired noble.

But he wasn't so sure about the lady in front of him. Her clothes were—well, they were what you would expect of a noble, but she didn't give off a "retired" vibe. Instead, she seemed like a matriarch, someone who was the real power behind her house, owing to her influence over the family head.

"Long ago, I never could have imagined such incredible amounts of information being gathered anywhere except in someone's head. However...," she noted, her words flowing like a river, "...it seems you hate tomes."

Her tone didn't seem to demand explanation, as though she was simply stating a fact. And she was correct. Ix remained silent.

"Well, I wouldn't know if you love them or hate them," she continued, "but it really is quite unfortunate. I have no interest in what you are searching for or why, but you are clearly hunting for information instead of books. Which is why you won't find what you seek."

"I don't understand…"

"Mm, I think it would be faster for you to look for something different or to bring someone along who can investigate in a different way."

With their one-sided conversation over, she tottered quickly away on restless feet until she disappeared among the stacks.

Ix sighed. As he thought about how difficult a conversation partner she was, Yuui approached from the bookshelves on the opposite side. Her arms were filled with new volumes.

"Um, what was that about? Who was that…?" she asked.

"The head librarian, apparently."

"Huh, really?"

"That's what she says." Ix shrugged, brow furrowed. "More importantly, were you hiding?"

"O-of course I would hide. I didn't know she was the head librarian, and… Well, you're the one who made me carry everything. Have you found anything on dragons?"

"Nope."

"So are those ones a wash?"

"Apparently so, because we're looking for information."

"…What is that supposed to mean?" asked Yuui, befuddled.

In the end, they wound up with nothing that day as well and went back home. They were both exhausted—Ix from all the reading he wasn't accustomed to and Yuui from all the books she was hauling around. It was only just past noon. Typically, they would keep at it until evening, but they had to leave early to help clean the shop.

Neither had the money to rent a place to stay, so they were both staying at Morna's. There were no beds, so they spent their nights sleeping on piles of rubbish like their host. It was getting steadily cleaner, though, thanks to Yuui's work.

Ix suddenly stopped while they were walking back.

"What is it?" she asked, turning around because she'd passed him.

"I remembered something I need to do."

"But we were going to help clean the shop..."

"It won't take that long. I just need to go check something."

"Really? All right, I'll go on ahead of you."

"Be careful."

"You too, Ix."

Yuui headed toward the old part of town, and Ix turned back the way they'd come.

He returned to the high-end area of the city, where the library was. Pedestrians thronged the streets, since it was noon, but eventually, the crowd slowly thinned. In their place, Ix began passing people in expensive clothing. In this case, expensive meant unnecessarily decorative. Ix wasn't used to clothing of this kind because he had grown up in a quiet mountain village. And sure, he sometimes added accessories to wands and staffs per customer request, but never anything that completely ignored practicality as much as those garments did. Despite how different wands and clothes were, Ix still found himself so interested in what these people were wearing that he couldn't help but gawk.

His first destination was the Wandmakers' Guild.

The Wandmakers' Guild was an organization that brought together everyone involved in the sale of wands and staffs, beginning with wandmakers. You needed their approval for gathering the wood or the core materials to craft wands or for operating a shop that sold them. It was rare for an organization to regulate a field encompassing only a single product on such a large scale, but that was testament to their high price and level of market penetration. Currently, however, the Adventurers' Guild was the largest of these groups.

As he'd mentioned to Morna earlier, Ix needed to register as a member of the Wandmakers' Guild. If they wouldn't accept him on the grounds of "cracking down on inferior wands," then he would be able to neither make nor sell the products in the field he'd been trained in. Although he'd momentarily forgotten because he was so focused on the dragon heart, Ix needed to become a craftsman soon, both to make a living from wandmaking and to fulfill Yuui's request. Until now, he'd been registered as an apprentice at Munzil's shop.

But the Guild immediately rejected Ix's application.

He hadn't known that you needed to already own a building that would serve as your shop in order to become a craftsman. On top of that, a new rule had been introduced recently that stated each store could generally have only a single craftsman. Large suppliers would need special permission to employ multiple artisans. Apparently, this stipulation had been put in place to bring down the production of inferior products, which could happen when a shop employed lots of "craftsmen" with barely any skill to speak of.

The Guild worker carefully went over everything with Ix, and then Ix left in low spirits.

"A shop..."

He didn't have enough money to own a shop. All his master had left him was enough cash to cover living expenses for a few months. He couldn't think of anything he could do to save up other than make wands, though.

One option was to work at a wand shop as an apprentice. Otherwise, he could get hired at one of the large wand shops that had permission, then get registered as a craftsman. He sighed. It was like his master had said. He was only half a craftsman if he couldn't get registered. It seemed it would be a while before he could stand on his own two feet.

Shoulders slumped, Ix headed for a district some ways off from the center of town to an area that had rows of shops aimed at the middle class. The good thing about the place was that it was full of energy. The bad thing was that it was squalid.

Though Ix had been nervous, since he didn't know the exact

location of the district, he quickly found what he was looking for as he walked down the wide street. All it took for him to reach his destination was following a trail of weapon stores and a group of people who seemed ready for combat.

This was the first time he'd set foot in the Adventurers' Guild.

The building was fairly large, but it was packed to the gills with adventurers regardless. Everywhere he looked, he saw leather armor, steel armor, swords, spears, bows, and the occasional wand or staff. The place was as busy as it gets.

Taking care not to bump into anyone to avoid being bashed to a pulp, Ix moved farther into the building. There, he saw numerous flyers affixed to a wooden board, each imprinted with a simplistic rendering of a magic beast, a price, and a location.

These are the request forms? he pondered.

He put some distance between him and the worked-up adventurers before peering at the requests in front of them. They all looked recent.

Since they would do him no good, he decided to go elsewhere. Toward the innermost wall of the building was the reception area, where male and female workers were assisting individual adventurers. A long queue had formed in front of each of the employees.

Ix watched them for a bit; there seemed to be quite a few adventurers here to report the completion of a request, so he wondered if they had to ask for a time slot beforehand. Additionally, it seemed that each member of the Guild's staff handled only a single type of job.

Resigning himself to the fact that this errand was going to take an unexpectedly long time, he joined the back of one of the lines. Almost immediately, an adventurer joined the queue behind him. Ix really stood out with his normal clothes and average build.

The line was long, but the worker dealt with each issue quickly, so it moved surprisingly fast.

Something caught his ear when there were only a few people left in front of him.

"What the hell is this about?"

"What I mean is—"

Some sort of argument was coming from the direction of the receptionist.

The room suddenly quieted. All the adventurers turned to look that way.

At the front of Ix's line stood two male adventurers, their arms crossed as they berated a female receptionist. Both were heavyset, with thick swords strapped to their waists.

"You got a problem with this?" shouted one of the men.

"These are the goods for the request, ain't they?" yelled the other, slamming his fist on the desk.

Meanwhile, the woman they were arguing with remained dispassionate; not even her brows twitched. She stared at them coldly. Though she looked young, she clearly had guts to spare. Finally, in an even tone, she responded, "That's all well and good, but enedo aren't known to form packs. We still have questions about how you gathered this many teeth in a single expedition."

"Then how do ya explain them? I don't care if you've got questions or not—it don't change the fact that the teeth are here."

"And all I've asked is that you wait. We are considering how to proceed."

"Yeah, but we've got plans after this. How you gonna make up for that?"

"I also told you that you need not wait. I will issue you a proof of confirmation so that it won't be inconvenient for you to return at a later date."

"That *is* inconvenient for us. Living day-to-day's the biggest upside to being an adventurer!"

"The Guild isn't concerned with how you live your life."

"What'dya say?"

As sparks flew between the adventurers and the receptionist, Ix noticed an old bag sitting between them on the desk. It was so big that it would take both arms to carry. White objects were peeking out of its open top.

According to their conversation, those were enedo teeth. Ix regarded them with confusion.

Enedo were large meat-eating magic beasts that were red in color and had fairly violent dispositions. They were famous for their large, curved teeth, which people liked to use as decorations.

Those, however…

Eh, whatever, thought Ix with a shrug.

The argument dragged on forever without a single indication that it would end soon. Annoyed, the surrounding adventurers started making a fuss, shouting for them to drop it already. The Guild radiated with hostility.

Just as Ix thought his errand was turning into a pain so it might be best to give up for the day, the adventurer behind him in the line suddenly started chatting him up.

3

"What do you think?" asked the adventurer.

"What?"

Puzzled, Ix turned around and saw a man smiling placidly.

The first thing Ix noticed was how young he was.

There was some boyishness remaining in his face, and he was shorter than Ix. Upon closer inspection, he had a muscular build but also still seemed to be growing, so he wasn't an adult yet. Despite his youth, the sword at his hip was held in a high-end sheath.

"Oh, apologies for talking to you out of the blue," he said with a bow, then repeated himself. "So what do you think about those two?"

"What do you mean by that?" Ix asked in return.

"You're not an adventurer, are you?" The young man looked Ix over. "Normal clothes, no weapon, and you don't seem to have much muscle. Have you come to put in a request?"

"Mm, something along those lines."

"I thought so. My name's Tomah. I'm in a party with some friends, but today is my turn to line up for reception. They didn't join me, since it's so busy. Ah, my friends are over there."

He pointed to a female elf and a male vukodrak talking by the wall. Both of them looked about as young as Tomah. The people near them shot the pair an occasional glare, while the other adventurers kept their distance.

Ix raised an eyebrow at the unusual combination. Elves had characteristically long ears, and vukodraks looked like humanoid wolves. Both races hailed from lands the kingdom had invaded long before it had taken over Lukutta. Although quite some time had passed since those territories had been subsumed into the kingdom, there weren't too many elves or vukodraks to speak of. They tended to draw inconsiderate stares, and some citizens looked down on them or treated them horribly.

While Ix did feel some slight curiosity about the group, he wasn't the type to actively pry into their affairs.

He wasn't sure how Tomah took his silence, but the boy did shut his mouth with an "Ummm."

"Oh, how about you give me your request?" Tomah joked.

"What are you talking about?"

"The Guild's commission fee's pretty high, isn't it? The requester covers the commission, which I think is a forty percent increase. But it's so convenient to use the Guild that most people have to. Still, there's nothing better than working directly with adventurers. Don't you think?"

"……"

Tomah held up his hands as Ix stayed silent. "Ah, no, sorry about that. I'm just kidding, of course."

"If you're looking to kill time, do it elsewhere."

"No, no, that's not it...," Tomah replied, expression turning serious before he pointed toward reception with his chin. "What do you think? Can you really hunt multiple enedo in one go like that?"

"Why are you asking me?"

"It's surprising how much more normal people know about magic beasts than us. I guess it's because they live beside them."

"And what would you do if you knew the answer?"

"Well, if there is some herd of enedo, then I'd make a lot off them," said Tomah, his gaze very eager.

"You want money?"

"Well, yeah... I've got a friend who had some things happen and needs some money... Anyway, do you have any info about enedo?"

"I'm not aware of any herds."

"Right... It's just, your reaction made it seem like you knew something about them. Are you an acquaintance of those adventurers, by any chance?"

Ix sighed, sick of how annoying this was getting.

"You don't get it."

"Sorry, I guess I jumped to conclusions..." Tomah sighed, his shoulders slumping.

"That's not what I meant." Ix lowered his voice. "I'm saying those aren't teeth they gathered."

"Huh?" Tomah's expression hardened. "What do you mean?"

"The cross section is suspicious through and through. Enedo teeth are hard, so normally you gather them by breaking them off with a metal hammer. You can also force them out with a sharp enough blade, but even then, the cross section would still be rough. They tend to break vertically, you see."

Enedo teeth weren't used as a core material, but they were sometimes used for decorations on a wand or staff, which was what Ix was remembering. It was a difficult material to work with.

"But those ones falling out of the bag there, their cross section is way too smooth," continued Ix.

"Aren't the ones sold at stores like that, though?" countered Tomah.

"Sometimes they turn out like that if the shop polishes them to make them look good, but that's for when they go on sale. That's probably what made the receptionist feel like something was off." Ix shook his head gently.

"So what are those teeth, then?"

"Beats me. They probably bought them from somewhere. I can't tell if they paid for them or stole them, but it's got nothing to do with me. I don't want to get involved in that mess…"

Ix suddenly realized everything had gone quiet. He looked up. The adventurers nearby were all silently staring at him. As he gazed back, his expression filled with dread.

Before he realized it, he and Tomah had become the center of attention for everyone at the Guild. Obviously, the receptionist and the two adventurers focused in on him, too.

"…Uh, just kidding," said Ix, shutting his mouth and turning his eyes away from their stares. But no one let it slide.

"Excuse me." *Of course* the receptionist would speak to him. "Could you please tell me more—?"

"D-don't go spewing crap like that, asshole!"

The two adventurers started shouting and drowning out the receptionist's voice. Drawing themselves up taller, they sidled over to Ix.

But as they did, a figure stepped in front of him, blocking their path.

"If you've got something to say, then say it from there! Or are you planning to lay your hands on a non-adventurer?!"

It was Tomah, roaring at the two. His shout was somewhat awkward but still loud enough to make you unconsciously shrink from him. The pair of adventurers flinched.

As they did, the other adventurers started raising their own voices in support of Tomah. Shouts of "Take it to the Guild," "Stop whining just 'cause you got made," "Send 'em over to me," and so on filled the hall.

Realizing they were outnumbered, the men backed off.

"Shut up! We get it—we'll set ourselves right!" one shouted. They grabbed the bag full of teeth and left the Guild.

Afterward, Ix skipped to the front of the line and was led to a room in the back of the building. No one really complained about that, which was a relief.

It wasn't a very large room. What it lacked in space, it made up for with high-end chairs. When Ix sat down, he felt himself sink slowly into the cushion. He was so unused to this level of comfort that he feared it would make him tense up.

"Thank you very much," said the receptionist from earlier as she sat across from him. She lowered her head and told him her name was Miisha.

"I'm sure you would've noticed once you examined them up close. And things could have gotten ugly if Tomah hadn't been there," said Ix.

"Who's that?"

"The adventurer who defended me."

"Oh, of course. I'll make sure to express our thanks to him as well afterward," she said, folding her hands in her lap. "There are the issues with the delegation, and we are short-staffed as well... Normally, we would have more knowledgeable employees handling reception duties."

"Delegation?" Ix repeated. That reminded him—the guard at the gate had also said something about Yuui being an early messenger for a delegation. "What is that?"

"Envoys from the east. Are you not aware of them? The ambassador passed through this town on the way to the capital. I heard it caused quite the uproar."

"I wouldn't know... I only just arrived in town."

"Regardless of their true relationship with the kingdom, we

are allied countries on paper. The Guild assisted by providing guards... We've also been giving them information regarding magic beasts in the area, so we've been overwhelmed..."

Ix nodded. He easily imagined that this group was a delegation in name only and was actually just a display of the people from a colonized country. He could easily guess what Yuui had been afraid of.

"Now then," continued Miisha, "did you have a request you would like to place today? I'll expedite your offer in addition to providing a small monetary reward as thanks for earlier."

"It's not a request. I want to see something."

"Go on."

"I want to check the unfulfilled requests."

"...What do you mean by that?" asked Miisha, puzzled.

"The solicitation forms out front are all recent ones, right?"

"Indeed. Our policy is to only display flyers less than a year old. We do store older ones..."

"Can I see them? You just need to show me to the storage room. I'll pay."

"I don't think it should be a problem, but may I ask why?"

"Why...?"

"Yes. There hasn't been anyone who's wanted to see them before."

"......"

"Oh, no, I apologize. It was simply my personal curiosity. May I take a moment to go confirm with my superiors that that would be all right?"

"...Yeah."

Miisha left the room.

Why am I...?

Ix hadn't been silent in response to her inquiry because he couldn't explain why. The answer was simple: He'd wondered if anyone had requested dragon parts in the past. Obviously, he didn't think those would have been fulfilled, which was why they might have been cleared out and filed away with the unfinished jobs. However, if the client was serious about their inquiry, they would have done research into dragons. And in that case, they might have attached some sort of explanation to their form, which could include details like region names or physical descriptions. If he read those, he might find a clue.

In reality, the reason he hadn't answered Miisha's question was because he'd interpreted her words in a different way: Why was he expending all this effort?

A wandmaker's job was making or repairing magical catalysts. It wasn't searching for the materials. That was best left to adventurers or merchants. There wasn't another craftsman who would do what he was doing now.

And all things considered, he wasn't even a craftsman. He was nothing more than a novice, a half-baked artisan.

That's exactly why I'm doing it, thought Ix, grimacing in self-loathing. Since he lacked the talent his fellow apprentices had shown, he would have to compensate by doing things outside his normal duties, like searching for wand parts.

That was all he could handle as a mediocre novice.

Perhaps that was why he'd accepted Yuui's request?

Did it all come down to the juvenile train of thought that if he completed a job meant for a craftsman, then he could think of himself as one?

Miisha returned after a short while.

"I have received permission. There will be no issue with you going through them. No fee required," she told him.

"All right. Where to?"

"Actually, allow me to show you the way."

As Ix followed along, he mused about how this drop-in errand had turned into quite the long task.

Their trip to the archives took them out of the Adventurers' Guild for a moment because the unfulfilled requests were apparently housed in another structure. After a brief walk, they came upon a short stone edifice. It was surrounded by other buildings, and there wasn't a person in sight. Only one of the other structures was open, and it appeared people were in the process of moving luggage in and out.

Miisha put a key in a large padlock on the door to the archives, then pushed it open.

"…This?"

"Feel free to look as much as you like."

She says *feel free, but…*

The inside looked exactly as you would picture a typical storage room. It was filled with all sorts of rubbish—stones, broken furniture, even rusted equipment. A musty odor wafted through the open door.

Against the wall stood a row of wooden shelves. They almost touched the ceiling, so a ladder had been attached. The shelves were jammed with more paper than he could have ever imagined. Ix thought they didn't have to store them quite so seriously.

"I'm heading back to the Guild. Please lock the door when you finish and stop by reception before you leave," said Miisha.

"Uh, sure," agreed Ix vaguely.

As Miisha returned to the entrance, her footsteps echoed throughout the archives.

Just before she left for good, she poked her head back in and said, "Of course, it's no imposition if you want to come here some other time to investigate as well."

"Right…"

"Now then, I'll leave you to it."

With that, she was gone. The door was still slightly ajar.

After gawking in awe for a moment, Ix finally pulled himself together and began investigating the request forms.

He skimmed through them in rough groups of ten-year intervals. The solicitations had gone unfulfilled for a variety of reasons, from magic beasts being too dangerous, to the location of the assignment being too far away, to the reward being too paltry.

Though he'd already half given up by the time he started glancing through the files, he readily found requests for dragon materials.

Just a bit of searching brought out request after request for dragon bones, dragon hearts, dragon eyes, dragon remains, and finally, even information on the creatures. Of course, the fact that all these flyers were here meant they hadn't been completed. To Ix's surprise, a significant number of these requests were from distinguished thinkers.

The majority of the forms contained no locations or drawings of the creature, only a reward amount. And the closer to the present you got, the fewer of these solicitations there were. It appeared that belief in dragons continued to wane as the years went by.

With that, Ix decided to limit himself to looking into requests from a while ago. The Guild didn't operate on the same scale back then as it did today, so there weren't that many unfulfilled requests. On the other hand, the flyers they did have from that time were harder to read, either because bugs had eaten and degraded them or because they were written in old-style grammar. At a certain point, Ix started to see jobs in the form of words carved into wooden boards in addition to the yellowed papers. Both types were difficult to interpret, so it took some time for him to decipher each one.

Out of all these forms, there was one that caught his eye. The reason why was simple—it was starkly different from the paper and wooden requests it had been sandwiched between.

The request was literally of a different color.

Black.

He touched it gently. It was significantly heavier than paper or wood, and the characters on it were white.

It was a thin sheet of stone engraved with the request. The smooth curves of the characters implied they had been carved out with magic.

"...What's this about?"

Ix had no idea why someone would use slate for the request form, since they were typically meant to be used and discarded. And they'd used magic on top of that. That detail implied the requester was likely of noble stock, which Ix found hard to believe. While aristocrats might use the Adventurers' Guild in modern times, it had been nothing more than a small-scale odd-job guild back in the day. It hadn't been the kind of place a noble would have occasion to interact with enough to put in a request. Everything about this was peculiar.

Hesitant before the strange slate, Ix dropped his eyes to the words written on it.

"A dragon…in Mount Agnas?" he murmured quietly.

Research Dragon Mount Agnas—that was what was written on the request form in preposition-less old grammar.

Ix had heard of Mount Agnas. It was a volcano east of Leirest, the city he was in, an active one that spewed black smoke into the sky even now. It wasn't that tall, but it marked the beginning of a large mountain range that stretched to the northeast.

The volcano contained special veins where one could mine agnasite, a stone that shared the mountain's name. A town named Agnasruze sat in the shadow of Mount Agnas. Despite its low population, the town was blessed with wealth.

Ix was well acquainted with agnasite, since it was frequently used as a core material in wandmaking. Unlike normal gemstone cores, a small amount of the mineral was capable of outputting a massive amount of power. Just recently, he'd employed it in the process of synthesizing the compound core.

You couldn't see Mount Agnas from this city, since it was hidden behind other hills, but on a clear day, you could trace a faint outline of the mountain ridge in the sky from the mountain that Munzil's shop had been on.

But…

…was there really a dragon on Mount Agnas…?

Ix had never heard a rumor like that before.

That wasn't to say it was impossible, though. According to the legend, dragons rarely showed themselves to humans, and it was completely unknown where they dwelled outside of those rare instances. It would make sense for them to stay deep in the mountains, where people didn't often tread.

Ix hunted through the request forms near that one, but there were no others about Mount Agnas or dragons. With that, he looked to see if the request had included the client's name, but it wasn't there for some reason. The reward was meager as well; it was miraculous it had even been accepted in the first place.

Nevertheless, the strange request form still caught his curiosity, not only because of its material but also because something about it made him nostalgic. He had no clue why it did, though...

Maybe I should go to Mount Agnas, he thought, before immediately telling himself to calm down. Even if he went, it wasn't as if he had any other clues to go off. All he'd found here was a suspicious flyer from God knows who. There was a chance it'd been put up as some sort of joke. How would he explain to Yuui that he just kind of wanted to go and check it out?

A shadow suddenly passed over the request form he held.

Looking up, he realized the light streaming into the storage room had disappeared at some point. The sky had darkened. It was now around evening time, with night soon to come.

"...Oh."

Ix finally remembered his promise to assist Morna.

He wrestled with it for a few seconds, but no particular solution came to him. They'd probably finished cleaning the shop long ago. He would be too late if he went now.

Well, if he was going to be late, then so be it. At least this way, he wouldn't have to bother trying to think up excuses or solutions.

Tidying up the scattered request forms, Ix left the storage room, then locked it as he'd been told.

If he didn't book it, the Guild would probably close.

As he dashed down the path, he suddenly heard a voice.

"Hey."

Two men appeared in front of him.

"...What's this about?" asked Ix.

"Don't give me that bullshit!" shouted one of them. "We're here to give some payback for before. You understand?"

"Payback?" asked Ix, confused. It was dark, so he couldn't make out their faces very well.

"If you're gonna pick a fight with an adventurer, you gotta be ready for some violence, yeah?" growled the man.

"I wasn't picking a fight, and I'm not ready for that," replied Ix flatly. "Do you want money?"

"Huh? We told you we'd take it out on you!"

"No you didn't."

"You quibblin' the details with me?"

"I'm not."

Ix stalled for time, keeping up the conversation as he remembered who these two men were. They were the pair with the enedo teeth.

He regretted giving in to Tomah and saying what he did back then. Turns out that he *had* ended up getting dragged into something annoying.

...Should I run?

No, he thought, rejecting the idea. They were carrying heavy-looking swords, and unfortunately, they were too close. Even if he turned and bolted in the opposite direction, it'd all be over once they grabbed his collar. Obviously, fighting was out of the question. There was no way he'd win, considering numbers and strength differences.

After considering it for a few seconds, Ix let out a heavy sigh.

"All right."

"Huh?"

"I won't resist. Just get your revenge," he relented, spreading his arms.

The two adventurers were momentarily taken aback but then looked at each other and grinned.

"The hell's with this guy?" said one.

"His noggin's gotta be...," said the other, striking his head with an open palm. "Eh, don't mind if I do accept the offer, though."

The second one's shoulders shook with laughter as he drew his sword.

Ix opened one of his hands.

"Ah, I forgot to mention—things'll be tough if I die. Just make sure not to kill me," he entreated.

"Huh? What the hell you doing?"

"I'm begging for my life," said Ix.

"...Shit. You don't know the value of a life, do you...?" spat the man, shaking his head as if disappointed.

"Do you understand what I'm saying?" asked Ix.

"Oh, I get that. What I don't get is your half-assed attempt at begging for your life."

"Right. That's unfortunate, then."

"Guess it's an unfortunate day for both of us."

Ix looked up the road. There were no signs of passersby. He couldn't expect help even if he shouted.

Just give up, he thought.

No question—he would lose in an all-out brawl. And it was his fault for not being cautious enough even though he knew the risks. If he really did kick the bucket, you could say he was just reaping what he sowed.

"Hey, you really going to kill him?" asked the man not holding a sword, anxious. "If you don't hurry—"

"It don't matter. I don't hate him that much. It's just, you know...," answered the other, raising his sword aloft, "...I dunno if he's the kind of weakling piece of shit who'll die even if I do hold back."

Ix saw the broad flat of the blade coming at him.

4

Yuui wiped the sweat from her brow and let out a breath.

"Huff..."

Her morning had been nothing but schlepping books around, and her afternoon had been nothing but moving beast corpses. At this rate, she wouldn't be able to raise her arms anymore.

She gazed around the room. Ottou was cheerfully carrying some carcasses, smiling. He always looked like that, so Yuui couldn't tell if he had more energy than usual or not.

Morna, on the other hand, was very easy to read.

"Huff, huff, huff..."

"A-are you okay, Morna?" asked Yuui.

"I'm...o...kay...," she answered, rolling out some logs before unsteadily moving them elsewhere. Her bangs were plastered to her forehead, making her look even more disquieting than she already was.

Though Morna was the oldest, followed by Yuui, and then finally Ottou, their physical capabilities were completely reversed.

If only Ix were here, mused Yuui. She didn't expect much from him physically, either, but they could have gotten more done with four people than with three.

"His errand must have wound up taking longer...," murmured Yuui.

Though Ix and Morna holing up for their research had resulted in the compound core, it had also led to an absurdly messy room. Additionally, just as Morna was about to return to crafting afterward, she predictably found herself unable to find the tools and materials she needed. Since she would inevitably need to organize things first, Yuui had offered to help. Yuui wasn't connected to the shop, but she had a good conscience, so she'd felt some responsibility.

By dividing the room into a magic beast section, a log section, and a tool section, they managed to get it back to its original condition. It didn't change the fact that it was cluttered beyond belief, but they didn't have the energy to keep going.

When they finished with a quick once-over clean, Ottou left the store, humming as he went. It was time for him to head home, since it was evening. Needless to say, he didn't bother with a goodbye. He never did pointless things like that.

Apparently, Morna, too, thought that was how it was supposed to be, because she didn't even thank him for his help. To be fair, though, that was probably due to being so tired that she lacked the energy to get the words out.

As if to prove this, Morna collapsed after the organizing was finished. After a while, she managed to crawl her way to Yuui's feet and addressed her in a dead-sounding voice.

"Th-th-th-thank...you."

"Of course. It was my wand that caused all this mess," replied Yuui.

"Y-you helped so much... N-now I can return to wand crafting."

"Yes, please make some good ones."

"R-right now...," muttered Morna, looking down at herself, "...I can't move my arms."

"A-ah..."

There was a pause in the awkward conversation.

After staring closely at each other for a while, Morna's face suddenly twisted into a grimace.

"W-w-w-w-w." She gasped while looking down. "W-weird, aren't I? I... I'm n-no good at talking or m-moving..."

"That's not...," Yuui started to say, before shaking her head. "That is true, isn't it?"

"...Yeah."

"You and Ix are unlike anyone I've ever met. You really are some strange people...rude as it may be to say..."

"N-n-no, it's the truth."

"Are all of Munzil's apprentices like you two?" asked Yuui. At this, Morna brightened up and nodded.

"Y-yeah. We're all weird."

"But why...?"

"B-because our master was bizarre..." Morna fiddled with her hair. "A normal person wouldn't apprentice under someone that way... Besides, a normal person could find somewhere else to work, so they probably wouldn't need to become an apprentice."

Yuui noticed that Morna was speaking naturally now, but she didn't interrupt.

"People like me can't live in most places...but in Master's shop, as long as you made wands, no one would get mad at you. He was crazy, but I knew from the beginning he'd be like that, so I had nothing to fear. You know, when I talk to people, I don't understand half of what I'm saying," she admitted quietly. "But yeah, I think the rest are like that, too."

"I wonder if...that's why," mused Yuui.

"H-huh? Why what?"

"Ix." Yuui sighed. "We've been going to the library every day, so a question suddenly struck me. Why did he accept my request?"

"Ummm, well—"

"I know—it's the contract, right? But the person who wrote it is dead. There's no one to punish Ix if he breaks it. And to enforce complete compliance even after his death... Was Munzil really that terrifying a person?"

"...No. Actually, I think it just comes down to Ixie, maybe. He listened to everything Master said... All the other apprentices knew when to ignore him or couldn't always understand him."

"Hmm, that does not sound great..."

"So yeah, it's not obvious...why he accepted the request, is it?"

"Even you don't know why..."

"A-actually, I don't think Ixie does, either."

"Huh?"

Yuui wanted to interrogate her more, but Morna had already stood, as though she meant to end the conversation.

"Talking makes me antsy," she said, sitting down at her work desk.

After doing the usual ritual, she immediately started crafting. She slid into work so naturally, it was as if she'd been doing it all day. It was as though her trade was a continuous thread inside her, one that never truly stopped.

It would have been wrong to interrupt her, so Yuui left the room as quietly as she could.

The shop was pitch-black.

She lit the remaining stub of a candle.

Ix still hadn't returned.

She felt a slight chill on her skin.

Why did he...?

She thought about him again.

Yuui could tell he wasn't motivated solely out of curiosity.

Of course, fathers and teachers weren't exactly the same...

But both of them were following the orders of a dead person...

So why did they keep it up?

And would they even be able to?

She...

Would he tell her if she asked him directly?

I wonder if he'll come back soon...

Yuui laid her hands on the table and rested her chin on them as she stared at the dancing flame.

Fatigue frothed up from within her body, rising in the direction of her head. The bubbles gathered, became a mass, and slowly invaded her skull.

"...Ah."

Yuui woke to the sound of a knock on the door.

Wiping the drool off her hands with her sleeves, Yuui tried to take stock of her surroundings even as her mind refused to get going.

The candle had gone out. Only a bit of light shone in through the window.

How long was I asleep...?

Moving to the window on shaky legs, she looked out to check the position of the moon. It was as if a hole had opened up in the night sky, obscured by fast-moving clouds.

It's still the middle of the night, she thought.

Her eyes hadn't adjusted to the darkness yet.

Eventually, she noticed a rapping at the door. It had been there the entire time, but she hadn't processed it.

For a second, she thought it might be Ix, but then she shook her head. If it were him, he'd be shouting.

Regardless, Yuui put on her coat. Stretching her hands out in front of her to feel for furniture, she edged toward the door.

After clearing her throat, Yuui spoke.

"Who's there?"

"...Yuui?"

"Ix?!"

"Yeah."

His voice was nearly a groan.

She threw open the door to find him standing there, his black-and-blue swollen face dimly illuminated in the moonlight.

"Sorry I'm late," he mumbled.

"Wh-what happened to you?!"

Ix began to collapse just as Yuui led him into the shop. She propped him up and sat him down gently in a chair.

He raised an arm and pointed to the doorway.

"...Thank them."

"What?"

She looked in that direction.

Yuui could make out three figures standing a short distance away from the store. They were tinted blue from the moon's light and casting vague shadows on the ground.

"They carried me here...and treated me," Ix informed her in a rasping voice. "I was attacked on the street."

"Oh no..."

She didn't know the details, but he'd told her enough to know these people had saved him.

It was so dark that she couldn't see their faces. She strained her eyes to look at them.

The area suddenly brightened, putting their faces and environs into clear relief.

But it still took a few seconds for her to process what she was seeing.

The three stood there staring in disbelief.

Two young men and a young woman, all around her age.

"Yuui...," murmured Tomah. "What are you doing here...?"

But Yuui couldn't get any words out. It was as though something had caught in her throat. Her mind went completely blank; she couldn't even remember how to breathe.

"Yuui?"

The low voice she heard from beside her finally brought her back to her senses.

Trying to get her raging thoughts in order, she gazed at Ix. He looked back at her quietly.

"It's nothing," she answered at last, working hard to maintain an even tone. She returned to the entrance and examined the three people before her.

"Y-Yuui...," gasped the other young man. His large doglike ears stood straight up, but she held her hand out to stop him from saying anything more.

"Tomah, Dann, Rozalia, I thank you for saving him," she said.

"Th-that's not important right now...," stammered the same man, Dann. "We were worried! You disappeared all of a sudden... But you're all right, thank goodness..."

"I have nothing to do with you three anymore," said Yuui.

©Enji

"It's late, so let's discuss this some other time. I can express my gratitude then."

"Your gratitude? Why are you talking like you don't even know us...?" asked Dann, his ears sagging sadly.

"In any case, it's time for you to leave."

"Leave? Does that mean you're staying here?" Dann wasn't letting it go. "If you're staying here, then we can, too—"

"This isn't an inn. They're just doing me a favor."

"All right..."

"Wands...?" said the girl in the group, confused. Occasionally, her long ears would poke out from where they were hidden in her hair. She looked up at the sign. "Is this a wandmaker's shop?"

"Yes, it is," Yuui said with a nod.

"What? Is this wand store important? Yuui, I know we don't have any connection as adventurers anymore, but we're still classmates at the Academy, and we can't ignore this. No matter how little money you have, you can't rely on this run-down place. I know you don't want to ask us for help, but—"

"Rozalia, stop," commanded Tomah as he placed a hand on her shoulder.

"But, Tomah," she protested.

"Ix is an excellent wandmaker. I told you, didn't I? He realized those teeth were suspicious with a single glance." Tomah shook his head. "And Yuui trusts this store, so it has to be a good one. Don't speak that way."

"...You're right. I'm sorry, Yuui," said Rozalia, bowing her head.

"Water under the bridge." Yuui's reply was curt.

"You really mean it when you say you'll make time to talk later?" asked Tomah seriously. "Will you promise to?"

"I don't lie."

"Right. Well, we'll take you at your word and leave it at that for today. We're staying at an inn near the center of town. It's the one with a bird carved on the sign… If you do come to speak with us…you'll find us there."

"Understood."

"Oh, and about Ix. Rozalia cast some emergency magic on him. He shouldn't be at risk of dying."

"He's lucky his brain wasn't mush," added Rozalia. "I closed all the dangerous injuries I could find, but it will take time for them to seal completely. And I could have missed something as well. Have him rest for the next two or three days and make sure to keep an eye on his condition."

"I trust your skill, Rozalia. Thank you," said Yuui.

"And finally…he dropped this." Tomah held out a bulging bag.

"I'll make sure he gets it."

"You're being pretty cold," grumbled Tomah, dropping his gaze before suddenly grinning. "Well, see you later, Yuui. Apologize to Ix for me, please."

The three of them walked away down the road.

Puzzled, Yuui traced where Tomah's gaze had been and realized he'd been staring at her right hand. She looked down and sighed.

"…Hah."

She released the tension from her shoulders. Right now, Ix took priority.

Yuui had been clenching her fist so hard, it had gone dead white.

5

After entering the library, Ottou took a few steps, then stopped in his tracks.

Yuui had been warned that the boy would be like this

beforehand, but she was still shocked to see it for herself. Taking his arm, she quietly led him over to the wall. Though he didn't resist, his eyes were glued straight ahead the whole time. Eventually, he started walking on his own. If what Morna had told her was true, he should be back to his usual self momentarily.

This whole situation had actually been Morna's doing.

While Ix's life wasn't at risk, his wounds were severe, so he would be bedridden for a few days. They were on a deadline, however, so Yuui had intended to continue researching by herself.

But during that time, Morna had announced she would be closing the shop for a while to avoid the attention of the people who'd attacked Ix. Since Ottou wouldn't have anything to do for a few days, Morna had suggested he help Yuui. Ottou didn't seem opposed, and Yuui could use all the assistance she could get, so she took Morna up on her offer.

Nevertheless, Yuui doubted that was the whole story. Perhaps Morna had closed the shop as a pretense for helping her out. Yuui couldn't be certain.

Ottou was frozen so perfectly still, he might as well have been dead. Apparently, he was always like this whenever he encountered a new place or situation.

He would certainly make for a strange sight for any onlookers. Fortunately, however, there were few patrons in the library, so they made it to their destination without too many stares.

After a while, Ottou blinked, as though he were waking from a dream, and stared up at Yuui.

"Ah, that's right, Ottou," said Yuui, sorting what she wanted to say in her head. "I'd like you to look for Agnasruze books."

"The town by the volcano where you can find gemstones," he replied.

"Yes, that's the one," she confirmed.

Without another word, Ottou slipped into the shadows of the bookcases.

"Oh..."

Yuui didn't even have time to tell him that there were only paper bundles and battered books that way.

Reflecting on their exchange, Yuui wondered if she'd said the wrong thing. Ottou's abilities were admirable, but she still didn't know how to make the best use of them. She wasn't confident that she could communicate with him the way Ix did.

As it was, he was like a diamond in the rough. She sighed.

Well, she at least felt better now that she had a clear topic of research, rather than something as vague as "dragons." Ultimately, they'd been set on this path thanks to what Ix had murmured when he'd regained consciousness briefly.

"Research Agnasruze."

That was all the direction he'd given them.

Yuui had no idea how looking into a town was related to a search for dragons. When she'd tried pressing him for more details, she only managed to get some broken, disjointed thoughts from him. Something along the lines of "There was a strange request," which meant nothing to her. Though she didn't really get it, she was hesitant to interrogate an injured man.

He might have just been rambling in delirium, so Yuui wasn't sure how much she should believe. But it was the only lead, or something even slightly resembling a lead, they'd found so far. Anyway, it felt as if they were trying to catch clouds. But she decided they might as well look into it, which was how they wound up coming to the library...

There weren't many books on geography, and the ones that were there were strictly regulated. The library had affixed them to stands so you couldn't easily move them.

Yuui scoured these texts for clues, but they mostly contained information on large cities. She couldn't even find anything on some of the regional villages in the kingdom.

It hadn't been that long since she'd started researching, but she was already feeling like giving up.

Surely this was the kind of thing they'd be better off asking around for in the city; they should be hitting up merchants and travelers, not poking around in the library.

But Yuui was haunted by what had happened to her in Leirest. It made her wary of reaching out to strangers. Still, no one had told her to take off her hood since she'd passed through the gates.

That's right... She didn't have time to be afraid of that.

If she couldn't get the wand repaired by the end of summer...

Yuui could hear that shattering sound again just thinking about it.

"A book on Agnasruze."

"Wh-what?" yelped Yuui, realizing Ottou was standing in front of her and holding out a book. She accepted it absent-mindedly.

It was less a book and more a bundle of papers with a cover. The handwriting on the front was so peculiar that she couldn't make out its title.

The text was quite old, and the paper was poorly preserved. The cover felt gritty and not from a lack of quality—it was coated with what appeared to be sand or dust. Yuui's fingertips whitened in the stuff.

"Um, Ottou, this is...," muttered Yuui.

"It's a book," answered Ottou.

"Says who?"

She flipped gently through the pages.

It appeared to be a ledger.

The interior was filled with columns of item names and numbers, in the same handwriting as the cover. It went on like this for page after page. Evidently, the text hadn't been well cared for, since the crushed remains of insects clung to its pages. Though there were a few notes here and there, they were uninteresting and didn't seem to have anything to do with the ledger itself. Just scribbles.

Yuui couldn't see why this thing deserved to be stored in a library. They'd probably just grabbed a stack of papers to fill the shelves.

©Enji

"Ottou, I'm sorry, but what is this?" asked Yuui.

"An Agnasruze book," he replied with his perpetual smile.

"No, that's not what I mean…" Yuui shook her head, thinking it was her fault this had happened, since she'd asked the wrong question. "What makes this an Agnasruze book?"

"Ash."

"Huh?"

"There's a volcano in Agnasruze. There is ash on the book. It's not ash from a fireplace—it's ash from a volcano. So it's most likely from there."

It took a moment for Yuui to understand what he was saying.

"Ummm, so in other words…" Yuui blinked many times. "This isn't a book *written about* that town but a book *that was there*?"

"Correct."

Thinking back, Yuui realized she'd asked him to find "an Agnasruze book." Her shoulders slumped. Her vague phrasing had messed everything up.

Regardless, he'd done well to find this in such a short time.

If Ottou's judgment was correct, this ledger had been brought from that town to Leirest for some reason, where it ended up filling the library stacks.

That was obviously quite incredible and intriguing, but…

"Ottou, I'm very sorry, because you did so well to find this, but…," started Yuui. Just then, however, the hand that had been idly flipping through the pages stopped.

For just a brief moment, the character for *dragon* had jumped out at her.

It was to the right of a line item about halni dye.

Just a few scribbled columns of characters written in the margin, unrelated to the content of the ledger.

Though the peculiar handwriting made it difficult to read, Yuui managed to get through it. It appeared to be a simple diary note.

...Will this year's dragon procurement commence without issue? Only two weeks remain until the festival begins, and there is idle talk that things are only half assembled... I told them I was unsure of entrusting them with this. It is odd how lacking in motivation young folk are these days. No drive, and they rarely join the gathering... Regardless, I shall inquire with the youngsters tomorrow. If I threaten them, perhaps they would come to understand the disaster this could be.

"Dragon...procurement?"

That was an impossible combination of words.

This ledger was indeed old, but it was written in Central Standard, which Yuui could read. It wasn't written in Kingdom Classical.

Which meant the document was only about two hundred years at the oldest.

But dragons went extinct long before that. The earliest estimates placed it over a thousand years ago.

The time periods clearly didn't line up. They'd found this ledger by chance, so she didn't think it was a joke or a lie. And if that were the case, then what was this ledger? Just some meaningless scribbles? But they didn't feel fake as you would otherwise expect them to.

She felt her heart leap.

This...was a hit, wasn't it?

Ix had told them to research Agnasruze. They found a book they thought had been in the town. Inside was a note hinting at the existence of dragons. There were still all sorts of things they didn't know, but Yuui didn't think this was just a coincidence.

The possibility that this would go nowhere still remained, of course, but they'd found this clue so quickly after having searched so hard beforehand. One half of her was telling her to keep calm, but the other couldn't help getting excited.

Yuui rushed to read the notes before and after that one, but they were just complaints about the writer's wife or talking about how cute their kids were.

Poring over the text to see if she could at least learn the writer's name, she found a signature on the back cover. It was written in even messier handwriting than the front cover, however, so Yuui couldn't read it.

Anyway, she needed to tell Ix about this as soon as possible...

They needed to investigate this document more. There might be something written in some of the other notes, not just that one.

Yuui sensed someone standing behind her and turned around to look.

"Oh, you've found it."

"Ah!"

"But you've brought a different companion today. I believe that may have been the correct choice."

The person rambling on casually was the head librarian. Yuui thought she'd hidden herself the last time the woman had been around, but apparently, she'd discovered Yuui anyway. Perhaps it was to be expected; Yuui had been coming every day.

"Um, what is this...?" asked Yuui, holding up the ledger.

"It's not in the library catalog," claimed the woman with only a single quick glance at it. "Must be some random papers used to fill the stacks."

"Ah, I thought so."

"Do you want to take it with you?"

"Huh? Y-yes, but..."

To be honest, she had been thinking of just walking out with it. She didn't yet know which trivial notes in the margins could hold another clue. And in order to show Ix, who was still bedridden, she'd have to copy each and every one of the relevant entries. She could get more done if she enlisted Ottou's help, but it would still take time.

Unfortunately, however, the library didn't actually let you take books out. Just as Yuui thought the head librarian had probably come over to remind her of that, she spoke again.

"You can take it. It's not officially in our collection, after all. I'll give it to you."

"Huh, a-are you certain?"

"Yes, yes. However, I do have one promise I would like you to make before you do."

"A promise? What might that be?"

"Books are meant to be read. No matter their content, it is far too tragic for them to go unread, for the book to simply rot away without anyone knowing what lies between its pages. I want to save that text from such a fate, so I would like you to treasure it, whether that means caring for it as it fades or entrusting it to someone else. I cannot give it to you if you won't accept that responsibility."

"U-uh…"

Yuui stared up at the ceiling. She hadn't expected taking a bundle of papers would involve so much responsibility. Were books really that precious? But the head librarian's gaze looked sincere.

Was Yuui the strange one for being unable to answer immediately…?

Her eyes wandered for a time.

6

It took four days for the swelling to go down.

Thanks to that girl Rozalia's magic, Ix had felt barely any

pain. Even so, he'd been burning up as he lay there, and his head had been hazy. He couldn't tell when he was awake and when he was asleep, but his recovery seemed almost too fast, considering the horrific injuries he'd sustained.

In an attempt to pay back the others for caring for him, he quickly rose from bed, then went to organize the cupboards and do other small chores. The noise he made while clambering around was enough to cause Morna to swing by.

"Oh, I-Ixie...?"

"Ah, Morna. Sorry for bothering you."

"N-no, it's fine. As long as you're better... Fyu-fyu...," she said, relieved. "Are you feeling okay already?"

"Well, I think I can move without problems now," noted Ix, lightly rolling his shoulders to show her.

"R-really? Good. Yeah."

"Where's Ottou? And Yuui?"

"Oh, they're in the shop. I-I'll bring them."

Morna returned with only Yuui, however. Her exasperated expression seemed to say, "You sure are lively for someone who just got up."

"So was there something you needed?" Yuui asked.

"Yeah, after we split up, I went to the Adventurers' Guild. And there...yeah." Ix met her gaze. "There I found something that seemed like a clue. If I remember, it was—"

"Agnasruze, right?"

"...How did you know that?"

"You told me. Don't you remember?" asked Yuui, shaking her head. "We can touch base later. I have something to tell you as well."

"Okay..."

He felt somewhat dissatisfied with her explanation but decided to just keep going with his story. Then Ix explained everything that had happened that night.

He'd collapsed on the side of the road, suffering from the horrible injuries the two adventurers inflicted upon him. The pair had made sure to pummel every inch of his body and had broken as many bones as they could. Ix had been so injured, he couldn't even call for help or stand up. Instead, he'd lain on the ground, shivering.

But since the two adventurers had raised such a magnificent ruckus, Tomah and his group, who happened to be nearby, came to see what was going on. Perhaps this was the situation's silver lining. Apparently, Tomah's friend Dann had heard the jeers and had gotten a whiff of blood with his excellent vukodrak senses.

The two adventurers turned tail as soon as they saw the three running toward them, but Ix was already at death's door. It wouldn't have been surprising if he'd died, had Rozalia not quickly cast healing magic on him. The elf's powerful magic and excellent technique had averted his fate.

Afterward, Tomah realized Ix was the person he'd spoken to in the Guild. Feeling responsible for the incident, Tomah had carried him all the way back to the shop. That was everything that happened that night.

"I owe them my life," admitted Ix. "And it was all because I wasn't being careful enough. I'm only here because I got lucky."

"Yes, I am glad you came out of it alive."

"Especially since there wouldn't be anyone to fix your wand if I dropped dead."

"...Why are you saying it that way?" Yuui glowered at Ix. "Do you not think it's rude to Morna and me, since we were legitimately concerned for you?"

"No, I didn't mean it like that, sorry. But who were those three? My memories aren't all there from after I got jumped, but it sounded like they knew you...right?"

"...Yes, I am acquainted with them."

"From the Academy?"

"Yes, from there."

"Strange combination. Both vukodraks and elves are in a

similar position as you, Yuui. Well, it happened at different times in history... But you're all still students at the Royal Academy and even working together as adventurers—"

"I would prefer not to talk about it," said Yuui curtly, cutting him off.

Ix shut his trap before he could ask another question. He'd intended to lighten the mood, but it seemed there was something going on. As it was, he didn't know her well enough to pry further.

"Right, sorry," he said.

"No, it's fine. It's just that I have no connection to them now, and I have no intention of working with them again. That's all," muttered Yuui quietly.

"I thought you said you'd make time to talk again?"

"Is that any of your business?"

"No...it's not." Ix shrugged. "I just wanted to thank them for saving me, that's all."

"Then this discussion is over," she snapped and cleared her throat. "More importantly, would you mind telling me about the clue you found? Why did you have me research Agnasruze?"

"Well, I didn't intend to force you into it...," he grumbled, before telling her about the strange request form he'd found in the Guild's storage and that it had said something about dragons and Mount Agnas.

"You say the characters were written with magic on a slate?" asked Yuui, crossing her arms. "That is rather perplexing. I do not understand the purpose."

"Well, that's all the clue was. It's strange, but nothing more than that. Thinking about it now, I feel like it wasn't that big a deal. Sorry my delirious ramblings sent you on a wild goose chase."

"Oh, I'm not so sure about that."

"Huh?"

"I did turn up one thing," she announced, then went to bring an old pile of papers over from the shelf. Ix raised an eyebrow in question. It was her turn to explain. Yuui told him how she and Ottou had found this notebook in the library, how it was most likely from Agnasruze, and...

"Dragon procurement...?" asked Ix.

"Indeed." Yuui nodded. "I don't believe it is a real dragon, but I have to admit I think it might be a lead, considering its connection to the request form."

"Since Ottou claimed it had been in Agnasruze, I'm sure he's right," mumbled Ix as he looked over the cover with confusion. "Festival Supply Accounts...Ega Fulmen?"

"Oh, so that's what it says. Ega, is that a name?"

"It's an old male name."

"Do you know him?"

"Wouldn't that be nice."

Obviously, Ix was acquainted with neither the man nor his family.

Tossing the cover aside, he gazed up at the celling.

"Hmm..."

"What's wrong? I thought we'd made a breakthrough. With this, our only option is to go check it out, isn't it? If we can meet this Ega person...," said Yuui breathlessly, seeming somewhat excited.

"It's a breakthrough, but..." Ix shook his head. "It's a gamble. It's safe to say our only lead right now is Mount Agnas. Agnasruze is far, but we could get there in two days if we go by stagecoach. But that's cutting it close. If there's nothing there, then that's the summer gone. I'd like to act with more certainty."

"But we've exhausted what we can investigate here. We've researched everything, and the two clues we've found both point to the same place... Could that really be a coincidence?"

"But—"

"Is it possible you are trying to use the fact that we have

found a clue as an excuse to extend the period for repairing the wand?"

"Of course not," Ix said with a snort. "What I was going to say is that there is one other major issue."

"I'm listening."

"Travel costs. I don't have any cash. We need to pay for transportation and lodging when we get there."

"Uh, that's..."

That wasn't an excuse—it was a pressing issue. Since Ix didn't know whether his career as a craftsman would pan out, spending large amounts of money on a free commission could end with him dying alone in the gutter. That wasn't an exaggeration, either. And if that happened, her request would never be completed.

As understanding dawned on Yuui, her grin soured into a frown. She certainly didn't have the extra funds.

While they were scowling at each other, they suddenly heard footsteps outside the room.

"D-do you need...money?"

"Ah?! M-Morna!" Yuui jumped slightly, then forced a smile on her face. "Y-yes, we do. We were just talking about how we don't have enough to travel."

"Hee-hee-hee, th-then take this..."

In her limply hanging arms, Morna was carrying a bulging sack. She dropped it to the ground in front of them, where it made a heavy thud.

Ix looked inside and muttered, "Huh?"

It was a massive sum. Well, perhaps not massive, but a decent amount.

"Morna, where'd you get this...?" asked Ix pointedly.

"Huh? Ummm, it was... Y-you dropped it when you collapsed."

"I dropped it? All this?"

"Ah, n-no, not that—it was the, uh, enedo stuff..."

"Oh, the teeth?"

She was referring to those teeth that the pair of adventurers had brought into the Guild. They must have dropped them in the panic that ensued while fleeing from Tomah.

"S-so I sold them...and made some coin."

"Huh? You sold them?"

"Y-yeah," mumbled Morna. Ix stared unblinkingly at her, but she averted her gaze. "Uh, was that...wrong?"

"No, it wasn't wrong..."

"W-well, if we held on to them, those people would come and tell us to give them back. So I thought it'd be better to turn them into money. I closed the shop and asked the merchant I always work with... Was that...all right? Foo-foo-foo..."

"I guess that's fine..."

Legally, it wasn't an issue. Since they'd already sold the teeth, the funds belonged to neither the two adventurers nor the person who originally owned the teeth, since the adventurers had obtained them illegally. The money belonged to Morna. And if her merchant managed things well, no one should be able to find this shop.

But that bag had contained *a lot* of teeth. Getting your hands on that amount of material was hard work. Morna had gotten a hefty return on investment from selling them, and whoever turned them in at the Guild would have netted a good deal of glory. And the two adventurers had lost it all to some half-baked craftsman... Ix actually felt kind of bad for them.

"This solves our travel money problems, yes?" Yuui said in realization, clasping her hands together.

"...Yeah. All that's left is if the customer wants to take this gamble," said Ix.

"Then there is no issue." Yuui smiled. "Right, shall we get going? It would be best to leave as soon as possible. Perhaps we should even leave tonight if your injuries are not a problem."

"Oh, then I'll get Ixie's bags packed!" cried Morna.

"What? Morna!" shouted Ix, trying to stop her, but she'd

already disappeared. "...And you as well, Yuui. Hold up. You made it sound like you're planning on going, too."

"What are you saying?" she asked, blinking in confusion. "Of course I'm going."

"No, not 'of course.' This is my assignment. You should wait here."

"But the thing is...we're going to find someone. You can never have too many helping hands for a job like that. And besides," added Yuui as she pointed to Ix's face, "who will fix my wand if you get beaten up again?"

His face was still wrapped in bandages.

1

After their journey in the stagecoach, they hitched a ride in a merchant's wagon. Two days later, Yuui and Ix finally set foot in Agnasruze. Their shoulders and backs ached on account of their forced-march style of travel and the poor sleeping conditions in the station. There had been better accommodation options available, but they were saving their money. Regardless, it had otherwise been a smooth journey devoid of magic beast encounters.

Ix stretched up his arms and bent his body, resulting in pops and creaks. The sky overhead was a pale gray.

"Ack...," hacked Yuui, inhaling the dust cloud the wagon kicked up around her as it left.

"You look exhausted," Ix noted.

"That was exhausting even for me."

"Well, that's what wagons'll do to a person."

"We have both suffered. And you had to deal with that bag...," she said, picking up her own luggage, which had been dropped from the cargo storage of the wagon.

Ix had brought an unusually oversize bag for someone traveling. It was so massive, they'd had to pay extra fare.

"It was a mistake to let Morna pack for me," Ix muttered,

dragging his burden along. "Guess that's what I should've expected from a shut-in who hasn't gone anywhere once in her life..."

"What ultimately ended up in there?"

"Most of it is daily necessities I could have bought when we got here. It's ridiculous... The rest is stuff I can't figure out why she would pack, like mending oil. I bet she just put stuff from her room in here on a whim."

"You might be on to something."

They'd rushed to catch a stagecoach, so they'd not had time to check the contents beforehand. On the other hand, Yuui had originally been dressed for travel anyway and had packed light.

But something else was weighing Yuui down besides fatigue— gloominess.

"Wow, what an enormous mountain!"

"You think? It doesn't seem that big to me."

"Oh, you probably can't see, Dann. It's hazy, but I can just make out taller mountains in the range that continues behind that one."

"Didn't we cover that in class?"

"Did we?"

The source of her distress was the passengers disembarking from the wagon behind theirs.

Tomah, Dann, and Rozalia, of course.

Ix looked at Yuui's profile, wondering if she might collapse again. She pressed her hands to her temples, perhaps from a head-ache, but she seemed to be hanging in there.

Yuui had been in a bad way ever since running into the three of them the first night of the journey. She'd returned to their room muttering, "This is a dream; it has to be a dream...," before collapsing on the floor. Ix went out to see what had happened, only to reunite with the three adventurers, looks of embarrass-ment on their faces.

As they told it, they'd seen Ix and Yuui rushing to catch the stagecoach. That had made them think Yuui was reneging on her promise to them, so they ran after the two and jumped on a stagecoach without even looking where it was going. That was how they'd ended up in the same station as Yuui and Ix the first night.

After Ix had explained the series of events to Yuui, she'd seemed to understand. Her heart hadn't, though, because she'd done nothing but sigh the entire way to Agnasruze.

Ultimately, using Ix as a go-between, the three adventurers swore they wouldn't try to interact with Yuui until they returned to Leirest. Yuui seemed to be trying to ignore them to the best of her abilities.

She urged Ix to get away quickly, and the two started walking down a wide street.

"Huh, what an interesting town," murmured Ix.

"How so?"

"It's monochrome. Or maybe Leirest is just too diverse in comparison..."

It was only a vague impression, but he sensed Agnasruze was the exact opposite of Leirest.

The buildings were large, but there weren't many people out on the street. Still, the place had a decent amount of activity, about as much as you would expect from a mining town. For some reason, though, it also had a tranquil atmosphere. It was as if you were looking at everything through a translucent sheet of ash-colored paper. There was of course the smoke from the volcano floating through the air, but there had to be more to it.

Suddenly, they heard a loud voice from behind them and turned to see the three friends having some sort of argument in front of a stall. Yuui's brow furrowed as she spun back around and asked, "What should we do first? Find somewhere to stay? Also, are any of your fellow apprentices in this town?"

"It'd be good if they were," replied Ix seriously. "For now, all we can do is search for Ega Fulmen or the Fulmen family. The cover of that ledger had the words *festival supply* on it, so he must've been connected with some sort of festival. We'll ask the people of the town about local celebrations or if they know anything about 'dragon procurement'... And if we can figure out the connection between Mount Agnas and dragons, we'll have something to celebrate. Things'll be a lot faster if someone happens to have a dragon heart."

"Sounds like our hands will be full... How shall we search? It does not appear this town has a library."

"I've got one idea: a place where we can learn about a few of those in one go."

"Oh, where is that?"

"Dunno, have to ask someone who lives here."

"And if they don't know?"

"Then I'm out of ideas."

"Sounds like it could be hit or miss... Though I suppose I knew that already."

"And if we have time after that, I want to look at Mount Agnas."

"Can't you see it just over there?" asked Yuui, pointing to the black shadow that towered just outside the town.

The mountain had a dignified presence that seemed to bear down from the other side of the houses. Its sharp curves were outlined by the rugged crags and trees standing on steep inclines.

"That's not what I mean. I want to actually go check it out," clarified Ix.

"You want to go into the mines? I've heard you're not allowed to enter any that are currently in use and that magic beasts come out of the ones that have been abandoned. That sounds dangerous."

"Shouldn't be a problem if I hire some adventurers as guards."

"Do you have that kind of money?"

"I do now," Ix said with a nod. "Depending on the cost, though, I might have to use the money meant for the return trip and wand repairs."

©Enji

"Oh my..."

"There's got to be some way... Ah."

A boy suddenly rushed around a corner and crashed into Ix, who managed to totter upright on his feet. The boy, however, fell to the ground. His patchy clothing was dirtied with sand, and blood dripped from his knees. Ix quickly checked his inside pocket, but nothing had been stolen.

"You all right?" Ix said as he loomed over the boy, who stared back silently.

"I-Ix! You're scaring him!"

Yuui bent over to look the boy in the eye, though her hood still hid her face.

"Are you all right?" she asked warmly. "I'm sorry—my friend wasn't paying attention."

"...I'm fine," he replied coldly.

"Can you stand? If you like, we'll walk you... Huh?"

As the boy went to stand, they saw a small red sparkle in his hand.

Yuui and Ix held their breath as they stared intently at what he clutched.

"Th-this is mine!" shouted the boy, noticing where they were looking and squeezing his fist tight.

"Where'd you get that?" asked Ix sternly. "Tell me."

"I found it!"

"Found it whe—?"

As Ix tried to interrogate the boy further, other kids' shouts echoed from around the corner the boy had popped out of.

"Hey, Henri! Don't run! You a man or what?"

"He ain't got a dad, so he ain't a man!"

The boy leaped to his feet when he heard their cries.

Then he compressed himself and hid by the corner.

Just as the other children appeared around the bend, he pushed off the ground with both his feet and landed a flying kick on the lead boy.

"Agh!"

"Take that!"

The lead boy fell backward into the kids behind him, dragging them all to the ground with him.

The impact also sent the boy who'd landed the blow tumbling down, but he was the first to get back to his feet. Turning to Ix, he muttered, "...Sorry I ran into you."

Before Ix could say anything, the boy dashed down the street like a rabbit. His form grew smaller and smaller before he disappeared around a fork in the road.

"I hope you die, you piece of shit!"

"We'll kill you, Henri!"

"Don't get full of yourself!"

A few seconds later, the other children picked themselves up and tore down the same street, hurling insults.

After they, too, disappeared, Yuui couldn't help but turn to Ix.

"That...looked like it, didn't it?" she asked.

"It was a beautiful red stone." Ix sighed. "But you can get shards of gemstones like that anywhere."

"Yes, I thought so, too. But..."

"Let's just think of it as a good omen."

"...Yes."

For a while, the two of them stared in the direction the boy had disappeared.

2

They set out to stock up on food and information. Ix went into a random store on the side of the road, with Yuui following behind. As she did, the store owner quickly called out to her.

"Ah, you there, please don't touch that."

"Hmm?"

Something had been placed up against the wall by the entrance, and Yuui had nearly brushed her back against it. She quickly pulled away.

"Please be careful," chided the store owner. "Those are important."

"O-of course. I'm sorry." She bowed.

While Ix chatted up the store owner, Yuui took the chance to turn and see what was so special, but there was only some old wood placed there. Three long sticks, to be exact. They looked sturdy but were blackened. She had no idea what they were for.

Losing interest, she looked around at the store decor, only to realize something suddenly.

"...Not a decoration in sight," she said.

"What did you say?" asked Ix, coming back with a hard-looking bread roll in each hand. He handed one to her.

"Now I know why this town feels so different from Leirest," noted Yuui as she accepted the roll. "This store's interior is the same as these buildings. Almost none of them has any ornamentation."

"Hmm? Well, now that you mention it..."

Typically, mid-range or high-end stores would sport extravagant ornamentation to show off their class and to prove that the establishment was profitable. Though you could call technically anything they put up "decor," the art they hung ran the gamut from wall carvings to paintings. There were all sorts of decoration types.

But for some reason, ornamented shops were the minority in Agnasruze. Instead, most of the buildings had barren facades. That was what made the city feel so quiet.

"It's because this town is New Order," came a voice.

"What?"

Ix and Yuui looked in the direction they'd heard it to find that the man running the shop was speaking to them.

"Have you not heard of it?" he asked, looking confused.

"I am aware that it is a denomination of Marayism...," said Yuui.

"Ah, what a knowledgeable girl," said the man.

"*Young woman*," corrected Yuui, though her hood was pulled far down, so you couldn't blame him for making an assumption based on only her voice.

"Ah, my apologies." He bowed his head slightly and put a smile on his face. "We New Order followers abide the scriptures more strictly and carry out our daily lives closer to God."

"What's that got to do with leaving shops undecorated?" asked Ix.

Yuui had of course learned about Marayism in the Academy, but the New Order wasn't recognized as a legitimate denomination by the state church, so she wasn't too familiar with it. Apparently, Ix wasn't, either.

"God commands us to devote ourselves to our occupation. For farmers, that's farming; for miners, it's mining; and for people like me, it is God's will that I run this shop. What that means is the fruit of our labor belongs to God."

"Fruit of your labor?" asked Ix.

"Farmed goods, ores and minerals, and, in my case, money."

"Your earnings belong to the divine?"

"Precisely. God only temporarily places the money I obtain into my possession. I can't waste that on luxuries and unnecessary things like decorations. We believers are meant to live pure and modest lives."

"Pure and modest... So you only spend significant money on festivals, then?" asked Ix.

"Festivals...?" The man's eyebrows crinkled. "A festival is the height of squandering."

"Huh?"

"We should loathe festivals above all else. Waste, luxury, and, most of all, debauchery... They bring nothing but evil, not an ounce of good. A festival would serve only to amuse the poor, and there is nothing gained from that. Since celebrations don't fulfill the occupations we've been granted, they go against God's will—"

"W-wait," interrupted Ix, holding up a hand. "There are festivals in Marayism. Like the Feast of Meat and Heaven's Worship..."

"Those are festivals of the Old Order," retorted the man with a snort. "But where in the scriptures does it say to hold them? They're a symbol of continual corruption—that's what they are. I don't know how it is where you hail from, but there are no events like that in Agnasruze."

"Has it always been like that?"

"Yes, at least as long as I've been alive."

"I see..." Ix stroked his chin. "By the way, we're looking for someone."

"Oh?"

"Have you heard the name Fulmen before?"

"Hmm...? No." The man looked as though he didn't understand.

Ix grumbled, then fell silent. He seemed even more annoyed than usual. Couldn't he have at least held that back until they'd left the store? Now the store owner was eyeing them suspiciously.

"Um...?"

"O-oh, thank you for speaking with us," said Yuui, hurriedly moving in front of Ix. "I apologize for him—he's a little strange."

"No, it's no problem."

"Let's go, Ix." She pushed his back and urged him to leave the store. But just as they were about to, she remembered something she'd been wondering about.

"Oh, regarding these...," she said, pointing to the wood near the entrance. "What are they used for?"

"Ah...those. What they're used for, you say...?" Surprisingly, the store owner looked dumbfounded. "They're not used for anything."

"Huh? But you said they were important?"

"Well, they've been in the house as long as I can remember.

My grandmother would get in a nasty mood and yell at me if I messed with them, so I just sort of placed them there... I honestly don't even know why myself."

"Huh..." Yuui was puzzled.

"Well, they're neither luxury nor decoration, so I thought it would be fine."

"I can tell that much by looking at them..."

They left the shop and walked down the narrow road. There was no sign of Tomah and the other two. Yuui wondered if they would just go back to Leirest.

"They don't have festivals...?" muttered Ix. "I didn't know there was something like that in Marayism."

"And if that's the case, what exactly is the Festival Supply Accounts? Was there a festival a long time ago that the shop owner just isn't aware of?"

"Probably. But..." Ix sank into thought.

If what the shop owner said was true, then they had already failed to locate the festival. On top of that, it cast doubt on whether the Festival Supply Accounts ledger had actually been written in this town. Maybe taking Ottou at his word had been a mistake...

Yuui decided to try changing the subject and said, "Some of the New Order's way of thinking sort of matches you."

"You think?"

"Yeah. The work is your life, and you don't care about earnings. Isn't that how a craftsman thinks?"

"Well, it's not like I want to be super rich...," Ix replied flatly. "But by their logic, the wands I make would belong to God. I don't want any of that. Wands belong to people."

"Hmm..."

Yuui remembered the boy from earlier, Henri.

The stone he'd been carrying was still on her mind.

Suddenly, she murmured, "Why did the dragons go away?"

"What are you talking about all of a sudden?"

"Oh...nothing." Yuui herself was surprised to have voiced the question, but she kept thinking aloud. "According to the legends, dragons were creatures with infinite magic and incredible physical strength."

"You mean dragon magic?"

"Yes. Apparently, they could materialize anything you could imagine. Compared with dragons, humans are just dust. But despite all that, I somehow always thought they died out because humans spread over so much of the world... Still, just why did they go extinct when they had unlimited magic?"

"It's strange, yeah... But they're just legends. A lot of weird stuff happens in them."

"Does the kingdom have any stories that explain their extinction?"

"Don't get so hung up on this."

"I know we cannot completely trust our leads, but we are seriously searching for dragons, yes? We might be able to figure something out if we think it all through."

"Huh... Well, I don't think there were any that mentioned a reason for their disappearance. All I know is their numbers dwindled. Aren't the legends everywhere like that?"

That was the same as what Yuui had heard. Besides, dragons were just something from a story, so didn't a certain level of inconsistency make sense?

Wait—something just occurred to her.

If legends didn't require consistency, then couldn't they explain the dragons' extinction however they wanted? By that same token, however, if all the legends in the world consistently stated dragons had gone extinct for unknown reasons, wasn't that proof in and of itself that they had really existed?

Well, it was just an idea. Instead, Yuui asked, "What do you think the reason was, Ix?"

"What do I think?" he murmured, then was silent for a couple of seconds. "Infinite magic and incredible strength don't come out of nowhere," he posited, speaking slowly. "When using a large amount of power, you have to burn a lot of fuel. I don't know where they got that in the first place, but maybe their source wasn't enough anymore."

"Then couldn't they just not use their power?"

"Hmmmm." It was only a theoretical discussion, but Ix thought it through seriously. With a severe look on his face, he replied, "It was probably a physical issue. The legends say dragons were the size of small mountains. Even if they didn't use their powers, simply maintaining their forms would require a tremendous amount of energy."

"Ah, I see."

Convinced, Yuui clapped her fist into her other hand. The small impact sent fine crumbs scattering from her bread roll.

Just then, a strong gust of wind blew in front of them.

Yuui braced herself, holding her hood in place.

The falling bread crumbs were swept up by the wind before they hit the ground, then appeared to vanish into thin air.

The gale settled.

"Yuui, you okay?" asked Ix with a cough from the dust he'd inhaled.

"...What if they were small?" asked Yuui automatically.

"Hmm?"

"What if dragons were not massive like the legends say but were actually tiny? Infinitesimally small creatures, like a grain of dust."

"So small they wouldn't need energy to maintain themselves?"

"Yes. And what if they are not extinct at all but are still alive?"

"That's impossible." Ix shook his head. "Then how did the people who passed down the old stories know dragons existed in the first place? Why'd they lie and say they were huge?"

"No, not like that. They were big a long time ago."

"What do you mean?"

"They knew they couldn't maintain their massive bodies, so they slowly shrunk themselves. They got smaller and smaller, until you could no longer see them."

"I feel like that theory relies too much on random assumptions..."

"But I have evidence."

"What evidence?"

"The core of my wand," asserted Yuui, and Ix looked at her questioningly. "This is what I think: The material used for the core of my wand isn't a *piece* of a dragon's heart—it's an *entire* dragon heart. With a heart this size, the whole body would only be about the size of a lizard. Long ago, they were as big as a small mountain. By the time Munzil obtained the core and made the wand, they were like lizards. And now, they are no bigger than a particle of dust... They've been getting smaller and smaller over time. If that's true, then they didn't go extinct. Instead, we can say they changed shape and are still living."

"That's... But..."

Yuui returned to her senses the moment she saw Ix's bewildered expression.

"Ah, s-sorry, it was just an idea... First of all, if that was what happened, there would be some record of it," she said.

"No, it was interesting as a thought experiment," he replied, nodding. "Dragons still being alive. I'd never seriously considered it. If that were true, then dragons getting so small it made it seem like they'd vanished would be a reasonable theory."

"Can you think of any other possible explanations?"

"None that are realistic."

"...Ah, like they're invisible?"

"That was one thought."

"You have another?"

"Well, if the exact opposite— Oh," gasped Ix, coming to a halt as he started to speak. "This is it."

"What?"

Yuui stopped, having walked a few steps beyond him. That reminded her—she still hadn't asked where they were going. She'd just sort of trusted Ix to guide her...

"An inn?" she inquired.

"No. I asked where this place was at the shop earlier. A place where we can learn everything in one go."

Ix pointed to a large, plain edifice that looked like a storage building. There was a small graveyard next to it, but it looked as if it hadn't been used recently.

"A church...?"

"Supposedly." Ix seemed perplexed. "Pretty plain for a church."

3

There were few people in the church.

The interior was large and open, since people gathered there for congregation, and it exuded stillness. Several well-to-do-looking worshippers were gathered near the entrance, engaged in some amusing discussion.

Like the city streets they'd seen so far, the entire church building seemed to reject decoration entirely. It was absent stained glass, paintings, carvings, or other artwork. The far wall was decorated with a wooden Marayist symbol and an old staff. Ix only got a glance from a distance, but the staff appeared to be of high quality.

It was normal for a church to have a staff. Munzil's shop had occasionally received requests like that. Not only were these simple decorations great for showing off, but the clergy also employed them for casting spells in service of the church followers. Magic skill was a must for becoming a member of the cloth.

The head of this church, referred to as a sage in the New Order sect, was a man who left a strong impression, what with his magnificent beard and flat, broad facial features. He introduced himself shortly as Ost Yuub as he approached Yuui and Ix calmly, his expression somewhere between blank and smiling.

"Hmm...Ega Fulmen?" Ost replied with confusion when they immediately began questioning him.

"Yeah. Or even just the Fulmen family name. You ever hear it?" asked Ix, his arms crossed.

"I haven't, unfortunately."

"It's someone who lived in this town," said Yuui.

"I am the sage who was assigned here. I would know who they are if they have accepted their purification since I've been here or if they are devout believers. But if this is about someone who lived here long ago, well, I only wish I could be of more assistance..."

"That's why we said we'll look ourselves."

"I do wish wholeheartedly I could cooperate," Ost said with a shake of his head, "but the purification records are significant items passed down through the church."

"We get that. We're just asking to see them."

"Yes, however..."

The earnest sage just wasn't letting up.

The reason Ix came to the church was to search for Ega Fulmen, of course.

When trying to locate someone, you had to ask the people passing through the area about them. That was probably a sure-fire way to do it, but they didn't have that kind of time. That was why Ix had hit upon the brilliant idea of investigating the church's purification records, which contained the names of all the people in the congregation who had undergone the ceremony, along with the date it had taken place. Depending on the individual, it might even have a date of death and a list of relatives.

Ega Fulmen had once possessed the Festival Supply Accounts ledger. In other words, he was someone of a certain standing, and there was a high probability he would be somehow connected to the church. If that was the case, he would have a prominent place within the purification records. At least that was what Ix had surmised. Considering there was no longer any festival and Ost didn't recognize the name, however, his assumption was starting to look less than promising...

As Ix continued interrogating the sage, the churchgoers by the entrance seemed to sense a quarrel on the horizon and vacated the premises. Ost must have come to the end of his rope, because he eventually put up his hands and relented. "Fine, fine."

"You'll show us?" asked Ix.

"Well, you do seem utterly insistent. Do you have anything with which you can confirm your identity?"

"Identity..."

"Yes, I do, sort of," interjected Yuui as she rummaged through her inside pocket. "I am a student of the Royal Academy. That must be an acceptable standing...yes?"

"Ah, a student. Yes, of course." Ost rubbed his hands together. "And then, you are—?"

"A wandmaking apprentice."

"An apprentice?" His brow creased. "Then do you have a guild card or the like?"

"No, only craftsmen can carry those."

"Then unfortunately, I will only be able to show the lady here..."

"Excuse me, I understand that we're asking something very difficult here, but is there really nothing you can do to allow him to accompany me?" asked Yuui. "Ummm, for example, could I vouch for his identity? He might officially only be an apprentice, but in reality, he is an excellent wandmaker..."

"No matter how excellent he may be, I still need some identification... By the way, under which craftsman did you study?" asked Ost.

"Munzil Alreff."

"What?"

"W-well, Master Alreff has passed away, so Ix is currently

working at the shop of one of Master Alreff's other apprentices…," added Yuui.

Strictly speaking, Ix wasn't working at Morna's shop, either, but he didn't refute her. Right now, getting access to the purification records was their top priority.

"An apprentice of Master Alreff…?" asked Ost with a quick glance toward the staff at the back of the church.

"I understand how you might be skeptical, but—," started Yuui.

"It's that staff," interrupted Ix.

"What?" Yuui and Ost both said at the same time.

Ix trotted nonchalantly farther into the church toward the staff. Then he stopped a few paces away and stared at it from up close, without touching it. As he'd suspected when he'd first entered, it was indeed a masterpiece. And it had clearly been well maintained over its many years of service.

"Excuse me, what are you doing…?" inquired Ost in befuddlement from behind Ix.

"This is one of Munzil's staffs," Ix informed him.

"Huh?"

"…Ah, it's sturdily made," continued Ix, his eyes never leaving it. "Was the junction point sped up to hold down the flexion rate? Master would do that."

"Um, excuse me?"

There was a tap on Ix's shoulder. He turned around to see Ost standing there, glaring at him suspiciously.

"Am I wrong?" asked Ix.

"Are you incorrect…? No, this is indeed an early piece of Master Alreff's, which he gave to this church. But just because you guessed right doesn't mean I can trust you. That's information you can learn by asking any well-informed member of the church."

"What are you talking about?" Ix narrowed one of his eyes. "That wasn't a guess or anything—that's something any wandmaker would be able to tell at a glance. I'm not trying to convince you I'm really an apprentice of Munzil."

"Then what are you trying to do?" asked Ost indignantly.

"I just want to convince you I'm an amateur wandmaker you can trust for a bit."

"Hmm...and?"

"This staff hasn't been used lately."

"Hmm? Yes, that's true."

"Its day-to-day maintenance has been perfectly carried out. But...you could only call it bad luck. Not even Master could have predicted this would happen."

"I do wish you would get to the point soon."

"The point..." Ix couldn't help sighing. He was loath to do this, but he convinced himself this, too, was necessary, so he stuck his hand in his bag. "Ah, for the love of..."

He produced a tiny vial. The yellow liquid inside sloshed about.

"What is that?" asked Yuui.

"Kesga mending oil," replied Ix, causing Ost to cry out hysterically the moment he heard its name.

"What did you say?! Ah, why do you have that?"

"Because I know a lady who's a bit..." Ix trailed off, shaking his head in exasperation. "Is this enough to buy a small amount of your trust, Ost?"

"Y-yes... Of course, you clearly appear to be a wandmaking apprentice..."

The clergyman took the vial and nodded many times.

Since the purification records were in the basement storage, Ost led the two of them into the church and down the stairs. The moment they descended to the narrow passageway, the stench of rotting flesh assaulted their nostrils. It seemed a portion of the ossuary was designated for storage, which explained the stench of death. The smell of mold and mouse droppings filled the stagnant air as well.

It was gloomy belowground, so dark that they wouldn't be able to see anything without a lamp. Ost, however, proceeded ahead as if used to the place, until he came to shelves fixed to the wall.

"This is it," he announced, taking large books and stacks of paper from the shelves and spreading them out on the table in front. "From here on are the purification records."

"And that includes all the old records?" asked Ix.

"Hmm? Yes, it does. This town has many devout followers. Naturally, that calls for a great deal of documents."

"Uh-huh."

"You may look through these at your leisure, as long as you don't take them out of the basement. It's not exactly a thank-you for the mending oil…but you have helped me quite a bit," said Ost.

"Thank you." Yuui bowed.

Ix and Yuui exchanged glances and nodded. They quickly went to work.

Faint writing clogged the old documents. The characters were incredibly small, and there were many places that had been written in a hurried scribble. It was a struggle just to read in the dim room. Ix swept away a silverfish and grimaced.

Having the same idea, Yuui said, "And I thought we'd escaped from reading, but here we are again."

"If only there were a magic spell to solve all this," mumbled Ix, holding his head in his hands. "We're doing something no one's ever done, so the slow-and-steady route is our only way forward. We won't know if we could have taken a shorter one until we've finished everything."

They heard someone calling for Ost from upstairs. It echoed a few times through the basement. He gave a short "If you'll excuse me," then ascended the steps.

The clergy wasn't just for managing the church. They also gave advice to members of the congregation and acted as mediators. Ost was probably juggling a few things at once.

Yuui stared intently at Ix.

"Don't stop. We don't have time," he hissed, holding up a ledger. "Let's divide them."

"Okay... By the way, what was that? The vial?"

"Oh, the kesga mending oil?" he replied as his hands worked. "Kesga is the name of the wood used to make that staff. You don't see it often, though."

"I know the name of the wood. But why did you have that... mending oil? Actually, I do not know what it is to begin with... And he was so grateful for it." Yuui skimmed the ledgers in the bobbing light of the lamp as she divided them up.

"It's the kind of thing you would be grateful for," explained Ix. "Staffs—or really any implement, staff or wand, that you channel magic through tens of thousands of times—inevitably start to flex and become unstable past a certain point. Though a small amount of warping only minutely affects wands, that isn't the case with staffs. If you can't keep the magic stable, the barrier collapses."

"That's not something you hear about often."

"Most staffs that have been used that much are just stored as pieces of art now. That's why you mostly hear about it at churches... Anyway, you use mending oil to fix the flexion when the staff warps too much. When you coat the wood with it, it becomes malleable for a short period, at which point you can make the necessary adjustments. But some woods require a specialized mending oil. Putting the wrong salve on them can break them in an instant."

"And because it's specialized, not much is made. Hence his gratitude," finished Yuui.

"Well, kesga mending oil in particular is actually a special case... One of the side effects of the Lukutta war was that the majority of the forests used in the production were burned. It's not being produced anymore. There's still some out there in storage, but the price keeps skyrocketing on the aftermarket. You can't really get your hands on it now."

"Right." Yuui's expression didn't waver. "Wait. Why did you have that with you? Something as precious as that?"

"...It wasn't me," answered Ix bitterly. "Morna did it."

"Morna...did what?"

"She put it in my bag when she packed for me. There was just a vial of kesga mending oil, right there."

"...A coincidence?"

"Well...she'd probably heard before that there was a staff our master made, a staff made of kesga, in this town's church. She might have guessed they'd need mending oil based on when it had been made and its location... I didn't tell her we were going there, but maybe she thought it would be useful and just chucked it in."

"Sh-she can predict stuff like that?" asked Yuui, blinking rapidly.

"No way... Or so I'd like to think," replied Ix, looking down. "But seeing as she just did, maybe she does have it in her."

"...Well, that is all well and good, but I wish she would have told us before we left."

"And this is why she's bad at follow-through," snarled Ix, his voice unusually angry. "She probably didn't say anything because she was worried about feeling uncomfortable if her 'grand prediction' turned out wrong or something. Seriously, she's got so much talent but goes around acting like that..."

Just then, a crashing sound cut off their conversation.

They listened closely but heard no other noise. Something must have fallen over upstairs.

They both sighed.

The two of them had just finished separating the notebooks from the rest of the stacks, forming two piles on the desk in front of them.

Ix crossed his arms. "What's the sorting criteria?"

"Time period," said Yuui quietly. "All the notebooks from more than about a hundred years ago seem newly made. I can't tell if they're...fake."

All this time, they hadn't been researching the names in the books but rather had been looking at the texts themselves.

The purification records from a long time ago should, of course, be old objects. But mixed in among the notebooks they'd fished out were documents that had clearly been made recently. Although they looked old at first glance, upon further inspection, there was obviously a difference in the state of the paper and the level of pest damage. Yuui and Ix had hunted through the volumes in the library back in Leirest, tomes both old and new. One glance at these notebooks made them feel as though something was off, and one touch told them they were spot-on. Thus, they decided to check that out before they began looking for Ega Fulmen's name. Once Ost had left, they'd started dividing the notebooks for that purpose.

Ix shrugged at Yuui's observation. "I asked him if the old documents were kept as they were. Either he lied, or he actually believes it... Of course, it could be the truth if they were just rewritten to recover ones lost in a fire or because they'd become too bug-eaten. Which means—"

"But there is no record to support that," countered Yuui, looking pensive. "What if this church wasn't established that long ago?"

"It's possible, but they wouldn't need to make fake records if that was the case."

"Well...it would have been the Old Order before, right? Perhaps when the New Order took over, they disposed of all the records from their rivals. Then they made these to cover it up."

"Would they really go to all that effort for no reason? They could just pick up where the Old Order left off."

"Hmm, then maybe it wasn't them, but—"

"Wait." Ix held up a hand to hush her.

The sound of footsteps descending the staircase echoed through the chamber.

They quickly broke down the two piles and lined them up as

they were, then flipped a couple open to a random page to appear as if they'd been reading the whole time.

"Anyway, something's strange," whispered Ix. "I want to look into the ledger, but we should investigate this, too."

"I agree."

In their rush to act normally, they'd kicked up a cloud of dust. They sneezed simultaneously.

4

A few days had passed since then, but their research progress was slow.

At the behest of Ost, Yuui and Ix were staying at a congregation member's home. It felt like nothing more than getting a roof over their heads, but they were thankful for it all the same, since the town appeared to lack an inn. That house became their base from which they investigated the purification records or went out into the streets to talk to the town residents.

But they hadn't found any significant leads.

No matter how much they read the purification records, they just weren't finding the Fulmen family name. They asked the people of the town, but of course there was no one around who remembered something that happened a hundred years ago.

"Huh..." The lady running the shop whom Yuui was talking with tilted her head in contemplation. "A hundred years ago, that would've been around when my granny was born. But Granny's mind wasn't all there, and she's passed now, so you couldn't speak with her even if you wanted to."

"I see...," said Yuui glumly, hanging her head.

"Oh, and you mentioned it before, but I've never heard anything about this town being Old Order back in the day. My family only moved here during my granny's time, which would be...uh, about seventy years ago now, but apparently, it's always been New Order."

Yuui had expected that response. She'd spoken to other townsfolk who knew more about the history of the town, but they all believed it had always been New Order. Obviously, the New Order had been established after the Old Order, so they must have meant ever since then. That had been over a hundred years ago.

She tried asking about festivals, dragons, and Mount Agnas, but she didn't get any information. All she got was "We don't hold festivals," "I don't know anything about dragons," and "A friend of mine is a miner; they just discovered a new mineral vein."

"It's not that big a deal, though," noted the shop owner. "They mine until they run into a wall. Then they search for a new vein. And if they find one, they dig until they hit a wall. Mining is just doing that forever and ever."

As Yuui left the store, she saw Ix coming back. They'd divided up the work, and he'd been asking around at a nearby store. "How'd it go?" he asked with a glance.

"Uh, well, this one wasn't really..."

"Ha-ha-ha, sorry I didn't know anything," admitted the shop owner, crossing her arms and looking amused.

"Th-thank you anyway," said Yuui.

"...This store doesn't have them," murmured Ix as his eyes swept the store.

"Whatcha talking about?" asked the owner.

"Sticks. The bundle of three."

Ix was referring to the mysterious sticks that had been placed by the entrance of the shop they'd visited before, a bundle of three long, thin branches with blackened tops. While asking around town, they'd learned there were other homes and stores that had them. Not in this one, though.

"Oh, those." The shop owner shook her head. "Only old shops and families have those. Recent transplants like mine don't have them."

"So it's proof you're from an old family?"

"No, no, nothing like that. I think they just set them out because they've had them around forever. They're not useful for anything, and I've heard a lot of families are throwing them away lately because they just get in the way."

In addition to the purification records, these decorations also struck them as a strange element of the town, but they were just sticks. Look hard enough in any village, and you were bound to uncover some sort of meaningless custom or culture.

"Ah, we'll be going now. Thank you for speaking with me," said Yuui with a bow.

"Nah, thank you. At least this town's got peace and quiet going for it. We don't really get visitors. It was fun," replied the woman, beaming.

They left and walked for a while, passing through a tidy neighborhood.

Though the shop owner had told them there was peace and quiet, that was strictly reserved for the upper-class areas, the neighborhoods of rich store owners and farmers. Leave this area, and you'd come face-to-face with the slums of the lower classes, which thronged with the poor and the homeless.

They walked through those neglected streets in deep contemplation.

This town was divided into two. It had taken Yuui only two days here to realize that.

Almost all the upper-class citizens were devout believers of the New Order. They found God within work, meaning they were prejudiced against the poor who didn't work or, in other words, people who couldn't work. They seemed to believe that those people weren't fulfilling God's will. They acted almost as if they couldn't see the poor.

On the other hand, you had the lower class. While they had taken their purification rites, few among them were ardent believers. This was another sore spot for the upper class, which amplified their frustration with the poor.

The two classes were separated and rarely interacted. On account of this split, there wasn't much conflict between them. It was peaceful, in a sense. The bullying they'd witnessed on their first day was the extent of it.

That was the kind of town Agnasruze was.

Yuui and Ix were investigating this region of town as well. They'd speculated that Ega Fulmen had perhaps been a member of the lower class who hadn't been purified, who would therefore not appear in the purification records. The only way they could prove their hypothesis, though, was to go around interrogating each and every person in the neighborhood. Neither thought this haphazard investigation would bear fruit.

In the end, they came up with nothing, just as they'd suspected. Yuui sat on the ground and sighed. When she looked beside her, she saw Ix scowling in frustration.

The pair was in a sort of small open square where two large roads crossed. Crowds of people passed by before them. The area bustled with people putting on performances or running stalls. Many of them were homeless people with no other profession.

"What's that...?" murmured Yuui.

"What's up?" Ix raised his head.

"It's just, that..." She pointed to what she was looking at.

The center of the square was mounded slightly.

No, it was a hill of brown sand. The strange thing was, despite all those people passing through, everyone made sure to avoid it. Like a boulder in a river, the mound formed a gaping, unnatural hole in the tide of people.

Yuui and Ix had passed through this square many times, but they'd never stopped to actually look at it. The townsfolk moved so naturally around the sand, it wouldn't have caught your eye unless you stopped to examine it.

"What's that?" asked Ix, wrinkling his brow.

"I don't know..."

"I'm gonna ask."

"Huh?"

Before Yuui could say anything, Ix had already taken off.

He found a man sitting near the edge of the square and struck up a conversation with him. Next to the man sat a gaudily colored instrument. He appeared to be a street performer.

"I'm taking a break," he said gruffly.

"That over there..." Ix pointed to the center of the square as if he hadn't even heard the performer. "What's that mound of sand? Why isn't anyone walking on it?"

"......"

The performer glared at Ix.

Yuui finally came over, since it looked as though things could take a turn for the worse.

"Ah, I-I'm so sorry! He's such an inconsiderate jerk. Please don't let him get to you..."

The man looked at Yuui in puzzlement as she rambled on. He seemed somewhat surprised to hear a girl's voice.

Ix blinked in confusion as Yuui glared at him.

"Ix, why are you always so rude?" she asked.

"I thought he meant he had time, since he was on break..."

"That wasn't what he meant..."

There was a short snicker.

The two looked in the direction of the noise to find the performer letting out a dry chuckle.

"All right, all right. Just don't argue like that in front of me."

"Oh, I'm sorry for the trou—," started Yuui.

"Don't worry about it. What was it you wanted?" He stood up and looked around the square. "Oh...the Fulmeninia?"

"Fulmeninia?" murmured Ix.

"Have you heard of it?" asked Yuui.

"Nope, never." Ix shook his head. "But it sounds like Kingdom

Classical. In Standard, it would mean something like 'eye of the mountain.'"

Yuui nodded.

"Oh, so that's what it means," the performer said, his eyes going wide.

"Hmm? U-uh, why are you impressed by that?" asked Yuui without thinking. "Did you call it that without knowing what it means?"

"Guess so... It's not just me—I doubt anyone is aware of its meaning." The man stroked his chin. "Besides, I don't really even know what that is."

"You don't? How about what it's used for?" asked Ix.

"Uh, well, to be honest, I can't think of anything it would be good for."

"Then why isn't anyone walking on it?"

"No clue."

"But you know the name?"

"Yep. Well, I don't know if it's a name per se; everyone just sort of calls it that, you know."

"Just sort of calls it that...," muttered Yuui in amazement. "Then there are no laws that forbid you from stepping on it?"

"Nope. Just sort of what everyone does..."

They followed up with a few more questions after that but didn't receive any noteworthy information from the performer. Yuui wondered if it really was just some vague rule.

Ix stood there lost in contemplation, hand over his mouth. Then he asked, "Right, so if, for example, the two of us went and stepped on it, what would happen?"

"What?" The man looked as if he honestly couldn't understand the words that had just come out of Ix's mouth. "Why would you do something like that? That isn't allowed."

"We can't?"

"N-no. Only an outsider like you could even consider doing that."

"All right. If I told you I'll pay you to walk on it, what would you do?"

"There's no way I'd do it," the man said with an annoyed snort.

"What if I asked someone else?"

"You're not going to find anyone who'd agree to do it, not in this town."

"Uh-huh." Ix nodded as though he'd accepted the explanation. "I've learned a lot."

With that, he ambled off, so Yuui bowed and thanked the performer.

"Sorry to bother you out of the blue…"

"What, you're not going to watch me perform?" the man asked, arching a brow.

"Uh, I thought you were on break?"

5

As they walked down a crowded street, Ix asked, "What do you think?"

"About what?" Yuui replied.

"Fulmeninia, Fulmen." Ix stayed facing forward as he spoke. "They're similar."

"Yes, I suppose so. In a children's wordplay sort of way."

"Fulmeninia, which no one will touch despite not knowing why. Three sticks, which are held in similarly high regard. Fake purification records from way back when. Then there's the Festival Supply Accounts book, which shouldn't exist, and Ega Fulmen, who wrote it." After repeating these observations aloud, Ix asked, "So, Yuui, what do you think?"

"Please do not push it onto me just because you have no

confidence in your own theory." Yuui sighed. "Not too long ago, you were chastising Morna for the same behavior."

"Fine, I'll tell you what I think, then." Ix frowned. "Guess I'll start with the conclusion... The evidence is flimsy, but I think there was an indigenous religion in this town a long time ago."

Yuui had also gathered as much.

Ix glanced quickly at Yuui's face, then continued.

"The state church was established about a hundred years ago. When that happened, clergy members were sent all over the kingdom. But since the New Order wasn't really recognized at the time, church members with those alternate views got mixed in among the missionaries. The Old Order strengthened, the New Order spread, and the church wiped out the local religions of towns that had previously exhibited no Marayist beliefs."

Ix posited that this town, Agnasruze, had met a similar fate.

"The mound of sand and the sticks are probably remnants of that old religion, though I can't determine whether they're tools used in festivals or idols to worship," he continued. "Even if you lose native beliefs, people's ingrained customs don't really change. The people here had acts of worship or taboos like 'You can't touch that' or 'You have to treat this with care,' and they didn't start breaking those rules just because someone told them 'Oh, by the way, you don't have to follow those edicts starting today.' Even with the advent of new generations, children grew up imitating their parents. They just kept on doing it this entire time."

"Traditions that continued even when they forgot their ideological roots?" Yuui smiled. "You may be bending some of the evidence to fit your theory, but I will give the rest a listen."

"That religion had a special festival, which Ega Fulmen was somehow connected to. But when the New Order sages came to town, the festival got erased along with the beliefs that birthed it. The Festival Supply Accounts book we found was most likely picked up then."

"Then why are the purification records faked?"

"To completely erase evidence of the old religion. After sixty or seventy years, the population of the city has been almost completely replaced, so there's no one left who can remember a time before the New Order. Now, the only thing that can speak truth to that past are records. That's why we were looking into them. From another angle, you could argue that the person who controls documentation dictates history. This town has been Marayist for a long time—that's how they want it to seem, at least. Normally, they wouldn't be so thorough about controlling that narrative."

"Was that religion popular, then?"

"Maybe it was the opposite." Ix put a hand to his chin. "For example, if the sages held all the power, then the citizens back then might have resented them. So they could have erased all traces of those beliefs to avoid angering them."

After a moment, he added, "If we believe the notes in that ledger—"

"Then that religion had something to do with dragons," finished Yuui.

The two exchanged glances.

Yuui wondered about Ix's theory.

She couldn't find any specific flaws with it. It seemed to have a certain amount of consistency... Well, no, she should calm down before jumping to conclusions. Sure, it was logical. But there wasn't enough evidence to make it convincing. They had so few clues to go on, and if you put your mind to it, you could make any random daydream match those few clues, free of any inconsistencies.

What Ix had proposed was speculation at best. It would be dangerous to convince themselves it was true.

With that clear distinction in mind, Yuui asked, "If your theory is correct, then what we're looking for was lost long ago. What would we do then?"

"Uh, well..." Ix trailed off. Perhaps he hadn't expected that question, because he couldn't come up with a response. "Right, well, we could go around asking the older residents..."

"Do we have that kind of time?"

"Well..."

How many old people were in this place anyway?

Discouraged, they stared glumly at each other.

The shadows of the square lengthened in the slanted rays of light.

"...Let's stop looking for today," Ix said with a shrug.

"Yes," agreed Yuui.

"You go on ahead. I've got somewhere I need to be."

"Hmm? All right."

They parted ways. Yuui set out toward their lodging but stopped after a moment.

This was how it had played out last time...when Ix had been attacked.

While this may have mostly been an excuse, Yuui essentially came on this trip to protect him. She didn't know what kind of errand he had to take care of, but this was Ix after all. The possibility of him getting dragged into another risky situation was absolutely on the table.

She turned on her heel.

Since she hurried back to where they were, she managed to just catch sight of Ix's profile as he disappeared around a corner. She rushed around the same bend, only to immediately conceal herself.

Ix wasn't alone.

Someone was walking alongside him.

...Tomah?

They were chatting about something.

Why were those two together...?

Yuui was baffled but remained in the shadows to trail them.

Eventually, they arrived at a quiet street and stopped. Yuui stuck close to a corner and discreetly observed their faces. They seemed very serious.

"Thanks for meeting with me," said Ix.

"Well, since you were the one who asked…," started Tomah.

Although they were far from the main road, the sound of their conversation nevertheless traveled away from them. Yuui focused and strained her ears.

"I'll cut to the chase," said Ix. "I want you three to help me, as adventurers."

"With what?"

"I want to venture into the Mount Agnas mines."

"I've heard normal people aren't allowed there."

"I'm not talking about going into one that's currently active. Instead, I want to go into one of the abandoned shafts. Word is that magic beasts prowl around there, so I want protection."

"Can't you put in a request with the Guild for this?"

"For starters, I don't have that kind of time. There's no Guild in this town, and I'm not in a position to sit around twiddling my thumbs to contact another city, especially since I don't know if there'd be anyone who would accept. Speaking of adventurers, you lot are already in town, ready to move at any time. You're convenient."

"So it comes down to 'convenience.' Any other reasons?"

"Saving money," Ix replied immediately. "There're magic beasts nesting in there, and all the ore has already been gathered. That kind of request has nothing in it for adventurers. No one would accept unless I offered a high reward."

"Which is why you circumvented the Guild and asked me directly?"

"Yep. You asked me before, didn't you? About direct requests."

"Yeah, I did say that, didn't I?"

"I don't have much left over after paying for lodging, but I can scrape some coin together as thanks."

"No, money isn't the problem…"

"I know I'm hitting below the belt asking like this," started Ix, not looking apologetic in the slightest, "but let me remind you, Tomah, that you were absolutely one of the reasons I got assaulted in Leirest. You said it yourself. Now I'm turning that misfortune into opportunity."

"…You sure are blunt." Tomah sighed with an uncomfortable smile. "If you're bringing that up, I don't have a leg to stand on."

"What do you think? You came all this way to Agnasruze. Why don't you help me out?"

"Hmm… Perhaps, but let me confirm something first." Tomah turned to the side for a moment. Yuui ducked her head back so he wouldn't see her. "Is this…to fix Yuui's wand?"

"Yeah. We've hit a lot of dead ends, and I can't think of anything else."

"All right. If that's the case, we don't need any compensation. We'll accept the request for free."

"I won't complain about that… But you sure? Don't you have to check with the other two?"

"Once they hear it's for Yuui, they won't be against it. Besides, I've got a pathetic ulterior motive: Maybe if she hears that I helped fix her wand, she'll soften her attitude toward me."

"Yuui said she doesn't want anything to do with you anymore."

"Yeah, well, things ended on a sour note… But I believe if we get the chance to talk, we can come to understand each other."

Understand…each other?

The moment she heard those words, a wave of weakness hit Yuui.

She lost her footing and wavered until she came to a squat.

"Yuui?!" she heard Ix shout. "Why are you here? No, wait, are you okay?!"

Tomah followed up with a surprised shout, and they immediately ran over to her.

Yuui placed a hand on the wall and stood sluggishly.

"I'm…sorry…for eavesdropping on your conversation…," she panted.

"Yuui, you're—"

"No, I'm fine. I was just surprised to see Tomah here…"

"Oh, I'm sorry…," mumbled Tomah, his expression clouding over as he apologized. "I'm sure you don't want to see the face of your family's enemy."

"Family's enemy?" murmured Ix. "Would that make you collapse on the spot?"

"Well, I—," started Yuui.

"Hold on, Yuui, I wasn't actually asking. Right now, you need to rest," Ix said.

Yuui looked at his concerned face and squeezed the breath from her lungs.

"Tomah and I, we…," she gasped.

"Yuui, don't talk! Take deep breaths."

"No, I want to…explain… I…"

Lungs emptying of air, bile rose in her throat as she forced herself to speak. Then she bent forward and somehow managed to hold it all back. But at this point, she'd wasted so much of Ix's time for her own selfish ends. With how far things had come, it would be dishonest not to tell him now.

"I'll… I'll explain," interjected Tomah, looking down with a severe expression. "It was the Lukutta war. My father commanded the invading army. His tactics resulted in the death of her entire family. Yuui has every right to be angry. Of course she wouldn't want to have anything to do with me…"

The boy's faltering voice grew distant.

Yuui sucked in air with all her might.

So he was still sticking to that story after all.

They'd talked so much, and yet, he still misunderstood…

"I apologize for worrying you," said Yuui, somehow managing

to wrestle control of her emotions. "Ix, you are going to investigate the mines?"

"Y-yeah."

"Then we should split our work... I will continue our research here. Please do be careful."

"Wait, Yuui—"

"I apologize for inconveniencing you with my personal issues. However, I request that you leave me alone."

As Tomah entered her field of vision, her words cut off.

"That's what I..."

With the rest of her statement caught in her throat and unlikely to work itself free anytime soon, she left them behind.

She simply walked alone, seeing nothing, hearing nothing.

Yuui feared that if she stopped moving, she wouldn't be able to start again.

After navigating haphazardly through the streets, she suddenly found herself lying in bed.

Memories she'd pushed far down in her mind burst loose and overtook her.

...Memories of nothing but screams and breaking.

Her mother, her brother, both gone.

They'd disappeared somewhere.

Only she had been saved.

Because her father had been there...

Her father had pulled her by the hand and led her to a secret cupboard no one knew about. There was only enough space for one. He told her to not come out, to not make a sound, no matter what happened.

And Yuui took the wand.

She didn't understand why her father had handed it to her.

So she asked.

Would he fight?

...He would, but there were other wands.

Would he die?

…He had no desire to die whatsoever.

Then why did he give her the wand?

…To which he answered, *"Because you, Yuui Laika, are the person most suited to wield it. Until I return, hold on to it and live."*

She thought he was lying.

Her father had meant to die, meant to leave her alone.

There was no other reason he would leave behind the wand that had become his symbol, the most powerful of its kind.

Yuui could vividly recall her father's face in the brief moment before he closed the door.

Those eyes, which reflected only his coming death.

…*Or not?*

In the expanse of her thoughts, something flickered.

…Had he really intended to die?

Or had he…not?

She knew that same face.

That's right… It was that one.

That expression…

The one Ix had shown her when he'd handled the wand…

As if finally remembering how to breathe, Yuui sucked in tiny sips of air.

Her body trembled; her diaphragm spasmed.

Her eyes throbbed.

She had been crying.

©Enji

6

The magic beasts in the mine had a peculiar appearance.

They resembled caterpillars that'd been given arms and legs, then made bigger. Although they were larger than a normal caterpillar, you could still cup one in both your hands. A group of about ten of them crawled across the walls and ceiling toward them to strike. They were surprisingly strong, and it took only a few of them to immobilize you. Still, they were lacking in the speed department. Easy pickings for an adventurer with a weapon. And though they flooded from the mines, no one had ever named them.

"...Hah!"

Dann swung his right leg, rending the underbelly of one of the beasts and sending it crashing into the wall. It didn't move again. He'd been felling most of the monsters that had appeared here.

Every once in a while, one or two of them would get past Dann, but they would quickly collapse beneath Tomah's sword. The adventurers marched on effortlessly, leaving a mound of corpses in their wake. Rozalia brought up the rear, never once letting her guard down as she scanned the area, though right now it didn't seem she'd have much opportunity to act.

Just as Ix had asked the night before, the three adventurers were acting as his bodyguards while he investigated the interior of Mount Agnas. Obviously, he didn't expect to find a dragon heart here, but there were some things you couldn't understand without seeing them for yourself.

The mine continued evenly for a while, then branched off into multiple paths. After producing a large map, Tomah pointed down one of them. Dann nodded wordlessly and forged ahead as Tomah used his short sword to scratch a sign into the wall.

The group operated in almost total silence and guided Ix in a practiced manner. This held true when enemies appeared too; the three worked so well together that you would think they had eyes in the backs of their heads. Despite their youthful facades, they bore the hearts of seasoned warriors.

After walking for a while, Dann spoke up for the first time.

"Phew, there's loads. Is it always like this?"

"No, I heard they barely come out in the active mines," replied Tomah. He'd gathered this information before setting out. "Once the mine is abandoned and people stop going in and out, the magic beasts start to nest like this. The townspeople just leave them be, though, since the creatures don't come out of the abandoned ones."

"Hmm..." Dann rolled his shoulder. "What do they live on? Don't see any food or water in this kinda place."

"The miners say they eat the holes."

"Holes?"

"Dann, you're speaking too loudly," snapped Rozalia.

"Yeah, sure, sure." Dann shrugged, waving his hand. "Now, what's this about holes?"

Tomah prefaced that these were just rumors, before explaining, "This mountain has had lots of minerals mined from it over the years. Once the villagers suck one vein dry, they find another. It just keeps repeating like that. Despite that, the mountain isn't full of holes. Apparently, there are no cave-ins, either." He pointed to the ceiling. "They say that happens because the magic beasts eat the holes and seal them up. And it's true that holes dug into the mountain quickly get dammed. The shaft we're in now has only been abandoned very recently."

"Ha, that's ridiculous. How can you get full from eating holes?" Dann shook his head and looked at Ix. "Ix, wasn't it? Whatcha looking for? You've been pretty quiet, but it's to fix Yuui's wand, right?"

The wandmaker's apprentice shrugged instead of answering.

"Keeping it a secret?" Dann said with a snort. "Fine, I wasn't gonna ask too much anyway."

"...It's warm," murmured Ix.

"Huh?"

"The wall."

Ix kept his hand on the left side of the wall. Though it appeared to be nothing more than cold stone, it gave off a slight warmth.

"That's...'cause it's a volcano. They're warm, right?" ventured Dann uncertainly.

"Really?" asked Ix.

"Well, no, I don't really know..."

"No, I'm curious. Did you learn about them in the Academy?" Dann's eyes flicked back and forth as Ix stared at him.

"I-I'm gonna go scout ahead!" yelped Dann, before hurrying forward. The light of his torch grew faint.

"Has Yuui said anything?" asked Tomah.

"No," said Ix. "She said to leave her alone."

Since they were walking single file, all Ix could see was Tomah's back. Tomah started talking bit by bit as they walked.

"Yuui came to the Academy over a year ago. It wasn't by choice. The kingdom forced her here from Lukutta." Tomah's voice was quiet, but it reverberated well in the mine, so Ix could hear it clearly. "She's the daughter of a tribe that is part of Lukutta's extended royal family. The kingdom called it study abroad, but that's just a diplomatic way of saying they took her hostage. They swore she'd be free physically, but she can't leave the kingdom of her own volition, and she can't own assets. She wasn't allowed to buy clothes. Naturally, the students at the Academy treated her terribly... That's why I invited her to join us."

"Join you? As adventurers?"

"Yeah. As you can see, we have a vukodrak member and an elven member. Might not be an appropriate way of putting it, but those three groups are in similar positions. I thought she might get along with them."

Both the vukodrak and elves were people whose lands the kingdom had invaded in times past. Though their former nations had been subjugated much longer ago than Lukutta had, there was no doubt that the citizens of the kingdom looked down on all three populations.

With that, Tomah continued his explanation.

"The Academy allows its students to become adventurers, but the compensation they receive from their activities doesn't belong to them—the Academy vault has rights to it. Then students are granted funds from the Academy. In kingdom law, that money isn't considered personal assets. So it's sort of a loophole, which allowed Yuui to spend her money the way she wanted."

"I see."

"I was surprised when she accepted our invitation right away. I asked her if she would find it unpleasant to get close to kingdom citizens, and she told me, 'I don't bring international disputes into personal relationships.' From then on, we were thick as thieves."

"That's the kind of person she is," added Rozalia from behind Ix. "She sees things more clearly than you could imagine. Sometimes she judges things so logically, it's scary."

"Logically?"

Ix glanced over his shoulder at her face. Her eyes wavered in the light from the torch.

"It's dangerous to look backward," she chided, and Ix turned around in compliance.

Tomah started explaining again.

"For a while, things went by without any problems. Yuui's smart and quick-thinking. She's good at magic, and she actually ended up saving us more often than not. And our adventuring let her make money she could use as she pleased, which made her happy. But..."

Tomah let out a sigh.

"It all started with the delegation."

Ix had heard about that somewhere. He racked his brain

for it. *Yes, that must be it.* "The delegation from the eastern peoples?"

"Yeah, that's it. They came from the east to the capital; we even saw them a few times at the Academy. That's when the topic of the Lukutta war came up... In hindsight, it was insensitive of me to talk about it in front of her. I think I'd gotten too used to how logical she was... No, that's just an excuse. Ix, do you know the strategy the kingdom employed in the war?"

"You mean, burning down every village and town they found and killing all its citizens...?" Ix had heard about it while in his master's shop.

"Y-yeah, you're well informed...," Tomah said nervously. "It was the only option. The Lukutta weren't accepting surrender, so the kingdom needed to make a decisive blow. Sure, it may have been possible to avoid killing everyone and slowly advance the war front, but that country is mostly forests. If the kingdom didn't thoroughly crush them, Lukutta could have attacked them from behind."

Tomah shook his head twice, three times.

"It was my father who proposed that strategy."

"And that's how Yuui's family died," Ix said in realization.

"Yes. They burned her village to the ground. Her mother and brother were killed in the attack, and apparently, her father traded his life for hers... It's heartbreaking."

"That's as horrifying as it gets," echoed Ix bluntly.

"Right after I brought that up, Yuui suddenly insisted she couldn't be around me... No, on second thought, it wasn't actually sudden. There's no one in the world who'd want to be friends with the son of the man who murdered your family. It's only natural," mumbled Tomah in self-deprecation.

"The elves were invaded generations ago," noted Rozalia. "So I'd never say that I can empathize...but I can imagine how she's feeling. Dann...he's not the kind to think about things too much, but he's worried about her."

"Well, you can tell that much just by looking," said Ix.

"So yeah. Her wand broke after that," said Tomah, back on topic. "We offered to pay for its repair, but she refused our offer. Then she disappeared when the Academy went on break, which—"

"Is when she came to me," Ix finished for him.

Tomah nodded slightly.

Only the sound of footsteps broke the silence.

Other than a short rest partway through, the group continued without issue farther into the mine. Tomah's map was highly accurate, so they didn't get lost.

Ix stopped several times to carefully examine the walls and floor.

The shaft went ever downward; as they advanced, the walls radiated more and more heat. Agnasite was scattered over the floor here and there, though all of it was too small to be of any use. They were most likely remnants of the mining that had once taken place here.

Ix gazed up at the ceiling, and Rozalia asked, "What have you been staring at for a while now?"

"There's no water."

"Hmm?"

"There are fissures in the ceiling and walls, but it doesn't look like water is leaking from any of them."

Instead of water, fine sand-like grains of agnasite streamed out from the cracks.

"Is that strange?" inquired Rozalia.

"No, I wouldn't go so far as to call it strange..."

Ix just had an inkling that this phenomenon was slightly different from what he'd heard about caves and mines or even volcanoes. He couldn't think of any connections to dragons, though...

Just as they were considering going back, they came up to a dead end in the shaft.

"This is one of those walls," deduced Tomah with his arms

crossed. "It's just like they said. Apparently, it's one huge sheet of rock that runs laterally through the mountain... If they run into this wall, that's the end of that vein. Then they search for another one."

Ix touched the stone as he listened to Tomah's explanation.

It was fairly hot. Not enough to burn you but definitely odd.

"...Dann, what is it?" asked Rozalia suddenly.

Peering over, Ix saw Dann inspecting the black wall just as Ix had done. But unlike Ix, Dann had pressed his entire body up against it.

"There's, like...a strange sound up ahead," said Dann.

"Sound? Isn't that just the wind blowing through the mines?" asked Tomah.

"No, it doesn't sound like it. It's a deep resonance, like a roar... Kind of like a river or a waterfall. And it smells just a little bit."

"Is it the stink of magic beasts?"

"No, not that. It's a heavy odor, but magic beasts smell worse. I have no idea what the heck it is. But I feel like I've sniffed it before..."

"Hmm, maybe it just looks like a dead end, but there's another mine continuing on the other side?" mused Ix.

Closing his eyes, he focused on what he could smell and hear, but he couldn't sense anything. Of course, he was no match for a vukodrak's senses.

Though he'd been pressed against the side of the tunnel for a while, Dann quickly started tapping it lightly.

"Hey, let's break it down," he suggested.

"Huh?" Tomah's eyes widened.

"We ain't gonna get anywhere just thinking. Break it down, and we can figure it out in one go."

"I guess that's true... Hmm," grumbled Tomah. "But how would we even break it? Is that even possible?"

"Well, if I go at it—"

"You can't be certain of anything. We have no idea how thick it is," interrupted Rozalia flatly. "But yes, it may be possible to disrupt it. I might be able to pierce through if I shoot it multiple times."

"...He was asking me," whined Dann, his ears drooping.

"Ix, what should we do?" asked Tomah, implying they'd think about that after checking with their requester.

"Hmm? Oh, well..."

Huh...?

A thought suddenly flitted through Ix's mind.

Agnasite from the walls and ceiling of the mine and this strange stone...

He felt a strong pounding through the wall.

"...No, it's impossible," gasped Ix, covering his mouth as he shook his head to and fro.

"What's wrong?" asked Rozalia.

"It's nothing..." Ix looked up. "Let's give up on tearing it down for now."

"Whoa, whoa, whoa, you made us come all the way here, and *now* you're chickening out?" Dann raised both hands. "I don't know what you're looking for, but there's clearly something here. You just gonna ignore it?"

"That's not what I'm saying. I want to get more information and some equipment before we make an attempt."

"But Yuui's wand repair—"

"I'm the requester," interrupted Ix with a frown. "Adventurers have a responsibility to do as their client tells them. Am I wrong? We have no idea what's on the other side of there. For all we know, lava starts pouring in as soon as we break it."

"That's rich, calling yourself a client when you didn't even go through the Guild."

"Keep it together, Dann," urged Tomah, stepping between the two. "What Ix says, goes. We should follow his lead."

"...Fine."

The four returned the way they came, leaving easy-to-understand symbols along the way so they wouldn't forget the route.

Ix marched in silence until Rozalia's voice came from behind, close to his ear.

"What did you realize back there?" she asked.

"What do you mean?"

"Don't play dumb. You had an incredible expression on your face."

"Just an idle thought. Not the kind of thing you talk about."

"Hmm, if you say so."

"Well, we'll know for sure if we see it. The next time we come."

"Next time will cost you money!" shouted Dann from the front. Apparently, he'd heard every word of their conversation.

"...Do you have money?" asked Rozalia.

Ix shrugged and kept his mouth shut.

7

"You seem worse for wear."

Yuui looked up to see Ost emerge from the gloom.

She brushed some dust off her hand. It was true that she looked ill. Being alone in the dim basement as she worked on checking the purification records was depressing work. That wasn't the only reason, though.

Ost approached her quietly, checking the flame of the candle. Then he murmured, "Seems it will last a bit longer."

"I appreciate your concern," Yuui replied very matter-of-factly.

"Where is your companion today? The apprentice."

"Ah, he had some business to attend to..."

The conversation finished there, but Ost didn't leave. Instead, he stood rooted to the spot, watching Yuui read through the purification records.

After a few fruitless pages, Yuui looked up.

"Ost…"

"Yes?"

"How long has it been since you came to Agnasruze?"

"Ah, well, this year will be seventeen years. I was in a different congregation before that."

"Seventeen years… That's quite a while."

"Oh, not at all… There are some who spend their whole lives in one church. I still have a ways to go."

"How has it been since you've become the sage here?"

"It's a wonderful place. Peaceful and pleasant to live in."

"From what I've seen," ventured Yuui, glancing briefly into his eyes, "the rich and the poor stand at odds."

"Ah…that." The clergyman sighed. "Yes, you are correct. This sort of division often occurs in New Order towns. But according to our tenets, all people are equal, regardless of whether they are wealthy or poor. I have explained this time and time again, but it seems the people don't quite understand… It's shameful—proof of my lack of skill as a sage."

His unexpected answer caught Yuui off guard.

"But this town has its merits," countered Ost, smiling and spreading his arms. "While it's true that this opposition exists, it never escalates into arguments or fights. Our population is made up of peaceful individuals, children and adults alike."

"Children, too?" Yuui asked, settling on a slightly malicious question. "The other day, some kids were bullying a boy…"

"Ah, that would be Henri." To her surprise, Ost responded immediately.

"You know him?"

"Only by name. He hasn't accepted his purification."

"…Is that the reason he's tormented?"

"I honestly don't know." Ost sighed, shaking his head sadly. "There are others who haven't been purified, but none of them are treated so horribly. Children will tease one another over the slightest thing, of course, but as to why him specifically…"

"Henri…"

Yuui fell silent.

She snapped the notebook closed and shot up.

"My apologies, I'll be leaving now," she announced.

"Oh? Ah, of course. Please come back again anytime."

"Thank you very much."

With that, she left the church and began investigating nearby.

While this place wasn't quite large enough to call a city, it wasn't a hamlet, either. Her only recourse was to search on foot.

Yuui headed toward bustling areas where children were likely to gather. That hunch alone wasn't enough to go off, however; morning gave way to afternoon as she searched.

Still, she continued to ask around as she wandered, until eventually she heard what sounded like the shouts of children and rushed in that direction.

Yuui came upon an alleyway with no foot traffic to speak of. Several kids had formed a circle and trapped Henri in the middle.

One or two of the children stood in front of him and tried to shove branches into his mouth. Each time they did, he would thrash violently, attempting to wriggle free. While the sticks didn't go into his mouth, they would stab his cheek instead and leave gouge marks, which made the other kids break out into hoots and hollers.

Yuui slipped her hand in her pocket as she moved closer.

"Excuse me," she called, and all the children whipped around simultaneously. "I have business with that boy. Is now a good time?"

They looked at one another, utterly confused, and started murmuring.

"Huh?"

"Who's that?"

"Some chick?"

"Please let him go," she demanded calmly.

Their murmuring eventually stopped, and all eyes gathered onto a single boy. He seemed to be the strongest of them. Realizing they were staring at him, he took a step toward Yuui.

"What's your business? Are you saying we can't be here?" he asked.

"I am. I'd like to speak with him privately."

"Hmm... I guess we could leave, but it's none of your business where we go next. We could just be nearby."

Yuui sighed.

"Huh? You got a problem?" the boy said with a smirk.

"Um, I'm sorry." Yuui shook her head. "I really should negotiate calmly, but it looks like that will be a pain, so I'll just use this."

"Use what—?"

Yuui brought out her wand and gently flicked it. A small orb of light appeared at its tip.

A shudder ran through the children.

"I-is that magic?"

"Uh, what do we do?"

They whispered to one another.

In reality, that orb of light had no effect other than illuminating the surrounding area. Yuui had been uncertain about using it, but the kids weren't used to magic, so it seemed plenty to scare them.

As soon as one of the boys turned tail, the rest of the kids scattered like baby rabbits.

Yuui watched them leave as disappointment welled up within her.

...*It's gotten so weak.*

This didn't even count as using magic. If the wand had been in perfect condition, it could have birthed an orb of light so bright it would blind you, so big it could swallow two or three houses.

Well, she could cry about it later. Instead, she walked over to Henri.

"Are you all right?" Yuui asked.

"Ah...thanks," Henri said with a groan, then looked away. "You want something from me...?"

"Yes, I do. I just have a little question."

An idea had struck her when she'd been talking to Ost.

If Ix's guess was right, if there really was some religion that had been wiped from this town in the past, then how would the priest of the old religion have been treated?

She didn't even have to mull it over. They would have been horribly oppressed, and those attitudes would be encouraged. If you didn't destroy the root of the old faith, a new one couldn't become established. In all likelihood, the priest would have been put to death, and their family wouldn't come out much better.

How long would those feelings have persisted? Would they disappear in a generation or two? Or would they cling to people for longer?

Would they remain like the town's baseless reverence for objects?

Persist like their nonsensical taboos?

Why was there a boy who kept getting bullied in this peaceful town? Ost, a relative newcomer, didn't know why. Which meant...

Though Yuui had been doing nothing more than desperately trying to fit pieces of this puzzle together, she nevertheless came to meet the boy to confirm her suspicions.

She cleared her throat, then asked, "Have you heard of a man named Ega Fulmen?"

"Ega? Never heard of him," Henri quickly replied with a shake of his head.

"Ah, really...?"

Of course, she thought.

Yuui must've been having a mental breakdown, grasping at straws like this, getting so worked up on a whim. As if something so simple would be true.

But just then, Henri continued.

"But I do know a Fulmen."

"Huh?" Yuui blinked. "Wh-who?"

"My grandma."

"What?"

"It's my grandma's name. Sheela Fulmen."

8

"Dann, we really should stop," urged Tomah as he stared idly at the shadows cast on the wall.

"But even if the wand gets fixed, we just did some bodyguard stuff. Yuui won't think we had anything to do with it."

"I'm not disagreeing with that, but our primary reason for helping fix her wand isn't to make her feel grateful toward us." Tomah sighed, exasperated. "And I don't know how I feel about not saying anything to Ix…"

"We decided by majority vote, Tomah. Stop complaining already."

"Might've been a majority vote, but that's just two to one."

"In other words, we have twice as many people."

Dann, Tomah, and Rozalia had returned to the mine shaft. They'd followed the symbols they'd left the day before and had made quick progress. The magic beasts were swarming again after only a day, but the group could move faster than last time, since they didn't have to protect someone else.

"You're being a worrywart, like always," grumbled Dann as he looked back. "All we're gonna do is open a tiny hole and peek in. We've got our equipment, and we'll split if it looks dangerous. Just like we always do. It'd actually be weird to bring the client with us."

"I guess…"

"Look, we're there already."

The three dropped their bags in front of the black stone.

Then they produced various pieces of equipment, like a sturdy rope and pitons to secure it.

To prepare for the possibility of water bursting out of the hole, they tied the rope around themselves. They had also brought a staff to cast a barrier spell in the event a dangerous magic beast reared its head. On the off chance lava spurted from the hole, they had all memorized the map of the mine so they could escape. They had considered these possibilities and many more— which had resulted in their excessive pile of gear. This was all due to Tomah insisting that they would proceed with caution.

"Right, looks good to me," announced Tomah with a nod after they spent time preparing. "Rozalia, if you don't mind. Just go bit by bit."

"I know."

Rozalia waved her wand, and a burst of purple light ran through the air.

It filled the dark tunnel with a brilliant flash.

Once the light faded, they could see a hole punched into the rock. Though it seemed pretty deep, it hadn't yet penetrated to the other side.

"Looks like we'll need a few more shots," murmured Rozalia.

"R-Rozalia, be more careful," stammered Tomah.

"Too slow. Hey, put more power into the next one," egged on Dann.

"*Sigh...*"

After processing the contradictory orders, Rozalia let loose another light pulse at almost exactly the same strength.

That, too, failed to pierce through. She hit it two more times, three.

Immediately after the fifth shot...

The moment the light faded.

The ground suddenly rocked.

"Whoa!"

Dann couldn't help crying out as he stumbled. He would probably have fallen were it not for the rope.

The earth heaved and rumbled, tossing him about.

As he lay on the ground in an attempt to keep himself still, he looked over at the other two. Both of them were gritting their teeth and enduring the tremors.

"What is this, an eruption?!" shouted Dann.

"I don't know! But we can't stay here! We have to leave!" Tomah shouted back.

Dann replied in agreement as he looked forward.

There was a hole in the stone.

The last hit had pierced through.

It was dark on the other side. He couldn't tell what was there… but that was only for a moment.

Something gushed out from the hole, and his field of vision was swallowed by darkness.

Before he realized it, he could no longer feel the floor.

"Huh?"

He looked toward the rope and the piton, but the piton had rushed off along with the floor.

Dann felt a strange floating sensation.

The next moment, he sensed that he was plummeting rapidly.

No, not falling—being sucked in.

"No way!"

He flailed his arms and legs, but there was nothing to grip on to.

He rolled himself into a ball and protected his head with his arms.

Then came an impact so hard, it knocked the breath out of him.

And then he was sinking into fluid.

He spread his arms and legs and raised his head above the surface.

It was so dark, he couldn't see a thing.

He was already being swept away by the violent flow.

Desperate, he stretched his arms out and felt something hard. He didn't know if it was stone or something else, but he grabbed on.

"Tomah! Rozalia!" he shouted, but the roar drowned out his voice.

He clutched the hard surface with all the strength he could muster, but his fingers soon grew numb.

"Shit!"

Was a river flowing on the other side of the stone?

A river?

For some reason, at the moment, he managed to collect himself and noticed something strange about this river.

It didn't feel or smell like any water he knew.

So what was it, then?

What was the thing most like this?

It was hot enough that it almost seemed to boil.

When he opened his mouth, the taste...

"Ah...?"

But he didn't understand the conclusion he'd come to.

He did everything he could to spit out the liquid that flowed into his mouth.

"Someone! I can't breathe!"

His fingers reached their limits, and the rushing river devoured him once again.

1

Ix crouched and examined the flower petals.

As he brought his face close, a faintly sweet fragrance reached his nose. He considered the insects clinging to the stems, then turned away.

Around him was the expanse of a flower field. Red petals flowed in scarlet waves whenever a gust of wind picked up. These flowers were called halni. They weren't especially rare and were often used for dyeing clothes and the like.

This area was just south of Agnasruze. If you looked north, you could see the plain rows of buildings and the outline of Mount Agnas on the horizon.

"Will doing this find us some sort of clue?"

Ix looked in the direction of the voice and saw Yuui coming his way looking frustrated.

He felt as if he hadn't seen her face in ages. Though she still seemed somewhat tired, it wasn't as terrible as she'd looked during his meeting with Tomah. Ix was glad she seemed better.

"Good job finding this place," he said with his back turned, concealing the relief on his face.

"I just asked Ost if there was somewhere nearby where halni were in bloom."

"There's a halni balance sheet written on the same page where the dragon procurement note is."

"I don't think that has anything to do with dragons."

"Well, it probably isn't much of a clue," agreed Ix. "But all we can do is investigate everything one by one. So..."

In other words, their investigation had really hit a wall. Even with how far they'd come, the only thing they had to show for their efforts was a single theory with weak supporting evidence, and they weren't getting any closer to a dragon heart. Seeing as they weren't able to locate Ega Fulmen in the purification records, contrary to expectations, they had only two lines of investigation left: continue to investigate Mount Agnas and—

"Looking into the festival. That's our only other option," said Ix.

"A festival that was held in this town long ago... But even if there was one, we can't prove that it has any connection to dragons," said Yuui as she spread her hands, palms up.

"We have no other hypotheses, so all we can do is follow it through." Ix sighed, shaking his head. "Festivals are usually established with a goal in mind. Usually, they start off more as ceremonies than festivals. But as the generations change, lots of people start participating, so it becomes more accessible and is refined into a real show. Sometimes it merges with celebrations from other areas. That's how their original meanings get lost. If there was a religion in this town centered on dragons, then the festival was probably a ceremony to worship them. And if we figure that out..."

"...Those aren't your own ideas, are they?"

"They're trustworthy ideas. It's something a scholar who visited my master's shop said."

"Well, good luck observing your flowers, then." Yuui sighed and moved away from Ix.

Since she was in the middle of a field of crimson flowers, it looked as if she was walking away across a red carpet.

According to what they'd heard, the New Order rejected things like dyes and luxuries. The vibrant halni seemed so out of place here precisely because they were juxtaposed against such an austere community.

Ix couldn't help but admire the beauty of the spot. Even though it was in the countryside, it would've been nice if more people were aware of it.

Actually…perhaps it was the opposite.

What if this place had faded only recently from the public consciousness? People harvested these flowers in the past. But they stopped using them, so the halni spread into an entire field. In that light, its presence could be supporting evidence for the theory that there had been another religion in Agnasruze. It was really just a thought, though…

After finishing his observations, Ix stood and looked around him.

Yuui had picked a flower and was twirling it in her fingertips. As he moved closer, she started speaking, as if to herself.

"It seems Tomah and the others won't be returning," she said with a sigh.

"I heard the same thing."

"The miners saw them heading toward Mount Agnas. No one has heard from or seen them since."

"So it seems."

"Do you have any ideas?"

"About what?"

"You know where they disappeared to, don't you, Ix?"

"What would you do if you knew?"

"What do you mean, what would I do…?"

"I'll tell you what I think happened, but it's all just an assumption. The other day, when we were investigating an abandoned mine, we discovered there was a strange sound coming from the other side of a dead-end wall. There, we discussed getting some gear ready to check out what was on the other side on another day.

After that, we went our separate ways. Then they disappeared. That's all I can say."

"Then that area needs to be investiga—"

"Investigated by whom? An abandoned mine filled to the brim with magic beasts? I can't do it. You can't, either, not without a wand. Would we ask some adventurers? Who's going to pay them? Or what if we try contacting their families? Even though we don't actually know that's where they went?"

"...It is not uncommon at the Academy for students to die or go missing when working as adventurers. But..." Yuui bit her lip and cast her eyes down.

"Besides, you hate Tomah, don't you? I mean, it's not surprising you'd break off a friendship with someone you got along with when you found out they were the son of your enemy."

Yuui looked up in surprise at Ix.

"Tomah told me the rest afterward," he admitted.

"...I see." Yuui closed her eyes. "I was sent to the kingdom as a 'study abroad student' because I am related to certain people. With my family dead, I was a very convenient hostage for the other royals. However, the color of my skin and hair was all it took to draw derision from the people here. No matter how much the kingdom pretends we are allies, its citizens regard the 'savage' people of the east, who don't believe in the same god, as lower beings, even when we hold no ill will toward them. If I was not covering myself with a cloak like this, I could not even walk around outside. The same held true at the Academy I was forced to attend, of course..."

"I thought the Academy accepted any who wanted to learn?"

That was the ideal it touted anyway. They swore to welcome all students who excelled, regardless of their social status or ancestry.

"It's a facade. Neither the teachers nor the students conform to that ideal. And I couldn't speak Central Standard, so to them, I was just an 'uncivilized student who couldn't even understand words.' The only people who extended a hand of friendship to me were Tomah, Rozalia, and Dann."

Yuui tore the petals of the flower to bits as she continued.

"They treated me as an equal. They were honor students as well, so the other students wouldn't touch me as long as I stuck with them. When we had time, they taught me the language. Everything I have now, my ability to live freely, is thanks to them."

"You're grateful."

"Yes, I cannot ever thank them enough." Yuui smiled and looked down. "...Then the delegation came."

"With the 'ambassador'?"

"I...couldn't watch. I am not certain, but it seemed the delegation truly believed what was just an act. It was ludicrous—how they gave the delegation a superficial welcome, how they made a show of exchanging handshakes, how everyone cheered loudly about how they'd deepened a nonexistent friendship. I was actually meant to attend the welcoming party as a study abroad student, but then I had that conversation with Tomah."

"He told me it was insensitive, that he shouldn't have talked about it in front of you."

"Well, they certainly aren't good memories. I don't remember it all clearly, just that the army came and killed my family and friends. People trying to flee were cut down one after the other... I had heard that Tomah's father was in the military, but to hear that he was actually the one who had proposed that strategy...yes, I was taken aback."

Yuui smiled painfully, but it didn't appear to be forced.

"But, Ix, that is not what hurt me. That's not the reason I broke off our relationship. I have explained it to Tomah many times, but he continues to misunderstand."

"So then—"

"It was because I realized we *could never come to understand each other.*"

Her coat flapped in a strong gust of wind.

"He told me that strategy was justified," she continued. "Claimed it was the right call because it brought the war to a swift end and reduced the overall number of kingdom casualties. But no matter how you try to dress it up, his plan was nothing more than the massacre of civilians. What do you think, Ix? Was that strategy wrong?"

"Depends on your perspective. From the kingdom's viewpoint, it was justifiable. From the Lukuttan standpoint, it was abominable."

"What about from an objective perspective?"

"Is there an objective perspective in war?"

"Yes, that is exactly it. That is all I meant."

Yuui looked up.

"We developed a friendship, our countries irrelevant; we fought together; we spent a year talking with each other. I believed we could come to empathize with each other somewhat. In fact, I thought we *had* come to that point. But that was impossible. I didn't understand a single thing about him, and he didn't understand anything about me... The moment I realized that—how do I explain it?—it felt like strength exited my entire body. And...yes, I fell into despair."

Yuui repeated "That was all" over and over.

"In the end, I got my own hopes up, and I let myself be betrayed. That is all. That was all..."

With the flower petals torn to shreds, she released them into the wind.

The red fragments spun and danced away.

She stared dimly at her hands.

Now empty, they had been dyed red.

It looked almost as if they were bleeding...

Bleeding...?

Ix held his breath.

That's it..., he realized.

He slowly let out a breath.

And then he asked.

"You felt despair?"

"Yes."

"Which is why you tried to get revenge?"

2

Yuui's eyes opened wide.

With trembling lips, she asked, "...How?"

"I thought it was strange," noted Ix. "That wand is amazing—it's the highest of high-quality catalysts. It shouldn't get damaged from normal use, and it should be nigh impossible for the core to shatter. That's what led me to believe there must have been a reason it broke."

"Which is...?"

"A wand's core determines its disposition. If the user isn't compatible, or if they try to cast a spell that's against their catalyst's temperament, then they can't use the wand's full power. Sometimes the wand will even bite the user back. Yuui, your wand has an unbelievably strong nature. It's unusual, even among the ones Master crafted. It would absolutely refuse to cast a spell that was against its disposition. No, it wouldn't just refuse to cast the spell. The core might just..."

Ix squeezed his fist, then opened it.

"Do you remember? What that wand's disposition is?" he asked.

"Incredibly...moral," murmured Yuui.

And the opposite of moral was...

But Ix continued without touching on that.

"My master was crazy, but he wasn't the type to make an impossible promise. He should have known that swapping out a dragon heart would have been a hopeless task. He would have known that repairing it would have been fruitless. So then why did he make a contract that stated he would mend it for free? The only conclusion I can come to is that he had another goal in mind."

"Another goal...?"

"So that if that wand fell into the hands of someone evil or was used for evil, then it would come back to him."

"...For what purpose?"

"You went to the shop. Didn't you see what was written on the door?"

Yuui searched her memory, but only a vague image came to mind.

"'Putting wands in the right hands,'" said Ix.

"Even a broken wand...?"

"Even a broken wand. That was Master's creed. That contract was a fail-safe, a way for him to get the catalyst back. A wand whose morality was the source of its power. We have no idea if the wands we craft are used to save people or kill them. That's up to the wielder—it's on them. But what we wandmakers can't stomach is an unsuitable individual casting unsuitable magic with our creations. You can't betray a wand."

"But... But that's not—"

"No matter what excuse you try to make, Master's wands are never mistaken. Yours broke because you did something immoral. Nothing more, nothing less," explained Ix coldly. "That's what it means to go against a wand's disposition."

He was right.

Yuui had known it was immoral, that it hadn't been justifiable whatsoever, but she'd cast a spell to get revenge.

And her wand had broken...and her revenge had failed.

"Don't get me wrong—I'm not judging you," added Ix. "The wielder determines what a wand is used for. Besides, I'm just talking about an assumption I've had. The contract didn't tell me to take back the wand, either, so I'll repair it and return it to you. It's got nothing to do with me if you then try to kill Tomah."

"Tomah?"

"Yeah, or maybe his father. Or that delegation. It doesn't matter who. Do you know what that means, Yuui? No matter who you try to get revenge on, it will fail. And you won't get it again."

"Get what again?"

"Even if I repair the wand once, I can't do it again. Next time, I'll ask for you to pay, and I probably wouldn't even be able to get the core material. What I'm asking is, do you really want me to repair it for you?"

Yuui realized what he was implying with that question. She couldn't respond with anything beyond "...How?"

"I've had an inkling about what the dragon heart really is."

"And you can repair it?"

Ix hesitated, then nodded.

Yuui gulped.

"Tell me," she entreated.

"Dragon heart is probably a mineral that makes up the core of the mountain and creates agnasite," mused Ix, hand covering his mouth. "Agnasite has been mined from Mount Agnas since time immemorial. But that normally wouldn't be possible. Mineral veins aren't some endless spring. They should have been depleted after decades of mining, but they haven't. In fact, there was agnasite pouring from fissures in the ceiling of the abandoned mine...like it was bleeding."

"You did say before that, rather than a dragon heart, you could use a compound core that contained agnasite for my wand. Is that why? Does something like that exist? A spring of stone?"

"The dragon heart is warm no matter when you touch it. That alone is strange. It's inconceivable that something can continue releasing heat perpetually without any input whatsoever. Either the dragon heart has lots of power stored in it or it has the ability to produce power itself. If there is a large crystal of that, it's a completely unknown gemstone. It's not unreasonable to assume it would have the capacity to create objects. Then it would actually be appropriate to call it a dragon heart..."

Ix shrugged regardless.

"Even if it does exist, it's probably buried deep below the mountain," he continued. "I have no clue how we'd get to it. But since that stone is in your wand, we know there's got to be a way. I'll find out how to obtain it before we're out of time, somehow."

"You sound none too confident about that."

"The thing is, Yuui, regardless of whether we can get the core material, the conversation still goes back to the question I asked before."

"Which was?"

"Whether I should repair the wand. You said that you need it before summer ends. I don't know what kind of spell you'd be planning on casting with it, but it will absolutely fail if it's for immoral purposes. Knowing that, do you still need it?"

"...Let me ask you something first."

"If I can answer, I will."

"Why did you accept my request?"

"...Because you came with the contract."

"Yes, there was a contract. But you had no obligation to comply. Your master is no longer here, and no one even knew what was on that agreement. I hadn't even read it. You could have just pretended it was nothing and torn it to pieces. Even if you hadn't predicted the repair would lead to this long and difficult journey, you, Ix, broke and only recently independent, did not need to accept the request. Am I wrong?"

Ix blinked a few times and hid his mouth with his hand.

"...That's right," he mused, an earnest expression on his face. "Tearing up the contract...that was an option. I'd never thought of that until you mentioned it just now. If I'd done that, I wouldn't have needed to deliberate over accepting it or not. Huh, you are smart."

"D-do not be impressed," spat Yuui, flustered at his unpredictable response. "Fine, so you are saying you accepted it simply because you did not think of another option?"

"No, I accepted it because..." Ix looked slightly up and murmured something quietly to himself, but then he eventually returned his gaze to Yuui. "Probably...because it was Master's order."

"Even though he's no longer here?"

"Well, you should still uphold those things," he continued, as if talking about someone else, perhaps not entirely convinced himself. "It's his last order, so I might as well listen to it. Besides, I owe him so much..."

Yuui looked at Ix, his brow crinkled in doubt, and felt her strength drain.

It wasn't a weak feeling like when she'd argued with Tomah. It was more like peeling off a heavy coat and tossing it aside...like when you've realized you've been unconsciously grinding your teeth.

She smiled.

"The wand will certainly break if used with ill intent, yes?" she asked.

"Hmm? Yeah, that's what I said."

"And my father would have known about that disposition?" she asked casually, trying as hard as she could not to appear grim.

But to Yuui, there was nothing more important than that. What was her father thinking when he placed that wand in her hand and left? That was all that remained within her.

Yuui stared with bated breath at Ix, who nodded.

"Of course. There's no way Master wouldn't have explained that."

After a few seconds of silence, Yuui nodded slightly.

"Thank you. Please fix my wand," she requested.

"For what purpose?"

"So that I can go save those three."

"Are you sure?"

"Yes... Surely that is a moral thing to do."

"A moral thing?"

—"*Because you are the person most suited to wield this wand. Until I return, hold on to it and live.*"

Even though those were the words of someone who'd already passed...

"I figured I 'might as well listen' to someone's last order," she insisted.

"I have no idea what you're talking about," said Ix, confused.

Yuui started off through the flower field without another word.

"Oh yes, I have actually found a clue in regard to Ega Fulmen," she added, turning back to look at him. "Though it might not matter now anyway."

"...That's not necessarily true."

For some reason, that was the only time the surly wandmaker showed a smile.

3

Ix followed Yuui back.

They headed toward an area on the outskirts of town. It was where the poor gathered, where all the dwellings were leaky and shoddily constructed. They saw dirt-covered children cut across the street. A bonfire sat to the side of the road, a gray liquid boiling in the dented pot above it. People crowded around the pot, heedless of the flies buzzing around them. There were no beggars. In this city, people avoided giving money to homeless people.

Yuui stopped in front of a haphazardly constructed stone house. It was slightly larger than the surrounding homes and appeared to have some history. Even so, it gave Morna's shop a run for its money.

"Is this it?" asked Ix.

Yuui knocked on the door without answering.

After a few moments, a hoarse voice replied, "Who's there?"

"I apologize for bothering you. My name is Yuui Laika."

"I don't know anyone by that name."

"I came because I would like to speak with Mrs. Sheela Fulmen."

"There's no one here with that name."

"Henri told me about her."

"……"

After a silence, the door grated open.

The wrinkled face of an old lady emerged from the darkness of the room. She was shorter than Yuui, and her stomach bulged out. Her back was horribly curved, and she moved strangely.

"What do you want?" asked the woman as she glared at them.

"Are you Sheela Fulmen?" asked Yuui.

"What if I am?"

"I'd like to ask you something," insisted Yuui.

"Ask me something? …And who's this other guy?"

"My name's Ix."

"What a rude man. Can't even bother to tell me your family name."

"I don't have a family name."

"Hmm, is that so? A lowly birth, then."

"Can we come in?" he asked.

Sheela snorted before shuffling back into the house.

The room was well lit thanks to rays of sun filtering through the cracks, but it still had a depressing air. Spiderwebs stretched across the corners, and there was no sign that the hearth had been used recently.

"I'm not giving you anything or nothing," asserted Sheela.

"That's perfectly fine," said Yuui.

The two sat on dirty rags spread across the floor. Sheela reclined in a large chair and let out a heavy sigh.

"So? Whaddaya want to ask of a poor, senile old lady like me?"

Ix opened his mouth to speak, but Yuui glared at him to stay quiet. She opened one hand slightly and launched into her question.

"I'll get straight to the point. Are you related to Ega Fulmen?"

"Where'd you hear that name?" asked Sheela angrily.

"So you know of him?"

"...That's Granddad."

"He was your grandfather?"

"Yeah."

Yuui and Ix looked at each other. They'd made a discovery.

"Now it's my turn to ask questions. How'd you hear that name?" demanded Sheela.

"From this," said Ix, revealing the Festival Supply Accounts ledger.

Sheela squinted and moved the text closer and farther as she tried to read the cover. Once she confirmed the title and author's name, she tossed it on the floor.

"Hmph, pathetic," she spat with a scowl. "His shameful notebook gets dug up long after he's dead and gets read by people with no relation... That's what he deserves."

"Um, your grandpa—"

"He was a worthless fool," hissed Sheela, taking a breath after every other word. "Was even worse when he went senile from old age. Got into gambling, built up a huge debt, claimed he would pay it off... They took everything from our home. If it weren't for him, then the house would be..."

Sheela coughed violently.

"So why'd you come asking about Granddad after all this time? If you've come to collect on his debts, I've got nothing left in here to give," continued Sheela.

"No, that's not it...," clarified Yuui.

"Who was Ega Fulmen?" asked Ix as he picked the ledger up from the floor.

"What do you mean?" Sheela frowned.

"As far as I can tell, your grandpa had something to do with a festival. But this town follows the New Order, and there's no sign of a festival here. The name Fulmen wasn't anywhere in the purification records. Who was he? And who are the Fulmens? Was there some sort of faith here before the New Order came to this town?"

"...I don't know anything about that." She clasped her hands together and looked down. "The New Order folk were already all over town when I was born. They threw mud at me whenever they saw me. I was never purified, and I never went to church. I always thought that was why they treated me so poorly, so I asked Granddad and my parents if I could do the ceremony. But they always ignored me. If I asked why, they wouldn't tell me... That answer your question? Hmm?"

"I don't get it," replied Ix. "Your grandpa and parents aren't here anymore. You should be able to get purified now, so why don't you?"

She gave him no answer. Instead, Sheela glared at Ix, a crease between her brows.

"You done with your questions? Then get out," she grumbled.

"Actually, we're just getting to the real reason we're here," revealed Ix.

"Hmph, you all like to prattle."

"There's a note in here about 'dragon procurement.' What does that mean? Who was your grandpa? Have you heard anything about this? Are there any legends about dragons in this town? Or something related to a different faith?"

"Dragons...," Sheela murmured, looking away and staring vaguely in the direction of the road.

Yuui and Ix waited in silence before she finally spat out a reply, as though she'd given up.

"The festival."

"The festival?"

"Granddad blabbered on about it day and night after he lost his marbles. Told us to get ready for the festival, talked about how preparations for it weren't complete, went on and on about this year's setup, yada yada."

"I knew it...," said Ix, leaning forward. "What kind of festival was it?"

"...What could possibly make you two want to know about the sleep talk of a senile old man?"

"Who cares—just tell us. What did he say?"

In a low voice, Sheela whispered, "Dragon Remembrance."

"Huh?"

"Dragon Remembrance... That's what Granddad called it."

"What happened during the festival?"

"Hmm... They'd make a giant dragon effigy and burn it. Sounds like a rubbish event to me."

"They'd burn...a dragon effigy?" gasped Yuui in surprise. "So then 'dragon procurement' was—"

"Probably getting the effigy ready. I don't know how much of it was true, though...," said Sheela.

Yuui and Ix looked at each other, lost for words.

The "dragon" was just an effigy. A doll.

Just something they used for a festival.

There was no doubt that the festival had been almost entirely forgotten by the end of Sheela's grandfather's generation.

The door suddenly creaked, and Henri entered the house.

He glanced at Yuui and Ix, then went into a back room without saying a word.

"So the bastard child's come back," hissed Sheela with scorn. "Unfriendly little brat."

"That's your grandson," chided Yuui.

"Not like I want to admit it. My daughter got knocked up at the tavern. Don't even know who the father is."

"And where is your daughter now?"

"Dead. Died in childbirth. Left me with a mountain of inconvenience..."

There were no doors or dividers between the rooms of the house, so her grandson had likely overheard her, but she didn't hesitate to say her piece. Yuui and Ix could just about see Henri from where they were, but he didn't move a muscle.

Ix readjusted his sitting position and cleared his throat.

"I want to know more about that dragon effigy. I don't care if it's only ramblings—just tell me what you know."

"You want to know...? What do you want to know?"

"Everything."

"What?"

"I want you to tell us about that festival in as much detail as possible. He told you about the preparations and planning, right? It doesn't matter if there are holes in the story—tell me everything."

"P-please, I would appreciate it as well," entreated Yuui with a bow of her head. "You are the only one left whom we can ask."

"...Are you trying to kill an old woman?" Sheela closed her eyes for a few moments, then spoke as if annoyed. "Fine, fine. I'll tell you what I remember. I don't know how long you two will sit there if I don't... Who knew a girl with a hidden face and a dreary man could make me feel so terrible."

"Th-thank you!"

And so Sheela told them.

With her advanced age and how long ago she'd heard the details, there were parts that were unclear, and she easily got off track. But when you put it all together, she essentially told them the following:

First, they would set up the Fulmeninia in a square in town, then pile up the sand and step on it to press it into place. It wasn't roped off or anything, but the citizens were strictly prohibited from walking over it.

On top of the sand mound, they would construct an effigy in the shape of a dragon. It cut a massive figure, as tall as two or three people, and consisted of straw and wood, things that burned easily, all tied together. Those were the preparations that would take place beforehand.

The morning of the festival, the town would be bustling with open-air stalls and people dancing in the streets. That was the only day when they were allowed to let their hair down, so there was an understanding that minor transgressions would be overlooked.

The main event was the burning of the "dragon." It was commonly called Sabineit Fulmeninia, which meant "light in the eye of the mountain."

A lottery would take place in the days leading up to the event to select a "person of purity," always a young child. After the person of purity was chosen, they would be forbidden from speaking with anyone other than the priests until the day of the festival.

When night fell that day, the townspeople would light bonfires. The lights would begin at the child's house and continue down the road to the sand mound.

"The bonfires were huge," Sheela told them.

A frame of three wooden sticks held the container for each bonfire, which made them as tall as an adult and ensured the flames would reach even higher. The fires were never allowed to go out during the festival.

Once midnight struck, the person of purity would leave their house and light a torch with the fire from a bonfire.

Then the child would walk barefoot through town while carrying the torch. No adults, or even friends, could accompany them. No one was allowed to offer any assistance.

When the child reached the mound of sand, they would light the dragon effigy with their torch. The townsfolk would gather in the square and watch in silence until it had burned completely away.

Then, after the flames had died down and they went to clean

up the remains of the effigy, they would find "treasures" in the mound of sand.

"Treasure…?" asked Ix. "Was that, like, gems or something?"

"I guess it was all lumps of gold," said Sheela.

"Lumps of gold… Where'd they come from?"

"They didn't come from anywhere. Someone probably buried them beforehand. How else would they show up?"

"Uh…"

Anyway, finding the treasure was the climax of the event, and the celebrations continued until the next day.

That was everything that happened during Dragon Remembrance.

"Granddad didn't even know when the festival started. But I guess he asked his granddad about it, who told him it used to be a calmer ceremony long ago," noted Sheela.

"Are there any legends or stories told about the festival? Like, with relation to dragons?"

"Hmm, I have no idea."

"I see…"

"Well, there're always those tales of adventurers killing dragons and stealing their treasure. Ridiculous that some moron would come up with the idea and pass it down like it was special. It's a good thing the festival's gone."

"The treasure, the gold," said Yuui, "who did it belong to? The child?"

"Yeah right. It went to the priest, of course. That was why everyone hated my family. The other townspeople accused them of keeping all the treasure for themselves and getting loaded off it."

"That isn't strange, is it? It was just the money returning to the people who buried it beforehand…"

"You think the people watching from the outside would be smart enough to realize that, huh?"

"From the outside…," murmured Ix.

"Don't mumble like that. If you don't want to be heard, then don't bother opening your trap in the first place. And if you got something to say, say it clearly," shouted Sheela, spittle flying.

"...Fulmeninia means 'eye of the mountain,'" said Ix.

"Huh?"

"Isn't that weird? Calling a small mound of sand like that a mountain."

"So what? Festivals are about making a big thing out of nothing anyway."

"Yeah, I guess." Ix shrugged.

As they chatted, the light coming in faded, and the room slowly darkened. It seemed they didn't have any lamps.

Yuui whispered to Ix that they should take their leave soon.

"Thanks for the information," said Ix, getting up.

"What a ridiculous pair you are, coming to ask about my senile granddad's prattle," Sheela said with a sigh.

"Th-thank you very much for taking the time...," said Yuui.

As they turned toward the entrance, the old woman suddenly stopped them with a bark.

"Hold up!"

"What is it?" asked Yuui.

"That book, Granddad's ledger...leave it here."

"Hmm?"

"He's dead, so that belongs to the Fulmen family. You've got no right to have it. Or do you disagree?"

"Wh-what should we do, Ix?" asked Yuui.

"Do as she says. Let's give it back."

He nodded and placed the paper bundle on Sheela's lap.

"Are you sure?" asked Yuui.

"I remember what's in it. There's no point in us keeping it."

"I suppose..."

Yuui looked at the old woman's face.

She was sitting with her hand on the cover, her eyes closed.

"Haaah..."

A sound passed through her lips, though it was impossible to tell if it was a sigh of grief or a groan of anger.

Sheela said nothing more.

"Let's go," Ix told Yuui.

"…What do we do next?"

"We get a dragon heart."

"What I'm asking is how."

"Listening to Sheela's story, there was one thing that stuck out to me…" Ix lowered his voice. "Not on the inside but the outside."

"What?"

"There are some things you can't get unless you go out, right?"

He looked sideways, toward Henri's room.

There was a small window, and Henri was staring out through it.

Mount Agnas towered on the other side of that window.

4

A forest spread out before them. When she looked up, Yuui could see the greenery gradually fade. The summit was shrouded in mist, leaving only a vague outline visible.

Yuui gazed up into a sky filled with drifting gray smoke.

She stood at the base of Mount Agnas.

"Let's go," said Ix, pulling up the cloth wrapped around his head to cover his mouth.

Magic beasts lived on Mount Agnas, but there wasn't an Adventurers' Guild in town, so it was dangerous to tread there recklessly. This also meant the magic beasts weren't really hunted, despite the mountain housing valuable lumber resources. A single path ran through the forest and continued partway up the mountain, which loggers bold enough to enter used occasionally. Fortunately, the foot traffic kept the trail packed down and free of weeds, so it was easy to hike on. It occasionally crossed with animal trails, but they didn't see any signs of movement.

Yuui scanned the area slowly, and Ix turned back to look at her.

"Don't be so on guard," he said.

"But magic beasts live here."

"In the higher elevations. They rarely come down to the lower parts. That's what the loggers said. Besides, I've got a bit of a defense ready for if they do happen to show up. You won't hold out if you're on edge the whole time."

"I can't trust any defense you concocted."

"Which is why I said you didn't have to follow me."

"I came because I don't have faith in your safeguards. Even weak magic should suffice for intimidation."

Yuui subconsciously felt for the wand in her inside pocket.

Walking up the mountain for the first time was surprisingly mentally taxing. Though trees blocked out the sun, sweat still beaded on her neck.

Weeds eventually encroached the path before it disappeared completely. Beyond that, the trees continued, along with waist-high underbrush.

"Looks like we'll have to cut our own path," stated Ix as he pulled a billhook knife from his bag. "As much as the townsfolk dig through the mountain, there aren't any who climb the outside of it. They all seem to hesitate for some reason. When I told them I was going to hike up it, they tried to stop me."

"Normal people would stop. A mountain covered in magic beasts is—"

"There are records of people who have done it."

"Is that so?"

"Well, most of them were daredevil explorer types. They'd climb to the top of Mount Agnas, then continue northeast along the mountain ridges...or at least they'd planned to anyway."

"Is there something in that direction?"

"I assume they were going so they could find out."

"Did they succeed?"

"Who knows. Those explorers never returned." Ix shrugged.

Once the path disappeared, their pace dropped dramatically. Ix took the front, wildly swinging his billhook, while Yuui held up the rear, guiding him. They wanted to take the most direct route to the summit, but considering they risked running into cliffs on the way, they couldn't just blindly aim for the shortest route.

Yuui grimaced, feeling disgusting from the sweat, small insects, spiderwebs, and sap coming from the cut weeds that caked her body.

As she sighed for the umpteenth time, Ix suddenly stopped dead in his tracks. She was surprised but quickly discovered the reason why.

"A magic beast..."

From the shadows of the bushes came a pair of long, twisted horns.

It was a magic beast called an illguna. Though they were timid herbivores, they could still pose a threat, since they would attack you unrelentingly if you upset them just once. Even seasoned adventurers hesitated to engage them.

But it wasn't just one illguna that had appeared. More horns burst from the underbrush, one after the other. Before they knew it, four of the creatures had surrounded them.

Four pairs of black eyes bore into Yuui and Ix.

A weak wandmaker and a student with a broken wand were at a disadvantage here.

But it might have been possible to strike suddenly and scare them. Yuui felt sweat run down her forehead as she quietly reached for her wand.

"Wait, Yuui," warned Ix, stretching his arm to the side, though he remained facing forward.

"But—"

"It's all right. Don't do anything. You'll still have a chance to use magic if they threaten to strike."

"...All right."

Yuui waited, her wand at the ready. She planned to immediately create a blinding light if they took a single step closer.

Beasts and humans stared at each other. Time passed.

"What...is going on?" asked Yuui.

The illguna neither fled nor attacked. They simply observed the two humans, blinking. Once in a while, they'd flap an ear up and down.

All that moved was the foliage around them and the bugs buzzing around the illguna.

"Uh-huh."

Ix seemed convinced by something and lowered his bag to the ground.

"U-uh, you are taking your sweet time...," stammered Yuui.

"It's okay. Look, they're not charging even if I turn my back."

"That does appear to be so."

Since he'd broken eye contact with them, all four of the illguna had moved their gazes to her. Yuui almost let out a small squeak but somehow managed to continue the staring match by herself.

Ix proceeded to remove a long, thin object from his bag. The whole thing was wrapped in paper and cord. He undid the knots to reveal a treated wooden stick.

"'Kay, Yuui, light this on fire," he said.

"Wh-what?"

"It's a torch. You can do that much magic, can't you?"

"Well, yes..."

Yuui looked between the illguna and the torch and frowned. At this point, she didn't think they would be able to drive them off just by holding up a torch. In fact, it could actually urge them to action.

Ix seemed not to notice her uncertainty. Raising an eyebrow, he whispered, "Hurry up."

"O-okay, fine!"

She flicked her wand and created a tiny ember. Holding it at the tip of the torch was enough to bring it quickly crackling into a blaze.

The moment the fire was lit, the illguna turned their heads away, as if shaken, before returning to their previous position and continuing to stare them down.

Ix raised the torch aloft and waved it slightly in front of him to show the illguna.

"I-it's not working…," noticed Yuui.

"You think?"

"We should run… Huh?"

Then Yuui blinked, unable to believe her eyes.

The illguna's noses twitched, they suddenly lifted their heads, and then they darted off into the forest.

It didn't seem as if they'd feared the fire. Instead, it was almost as if they'd suddenly lost interest and left them at once.

"You take this. Don't set the forest alight," urged Ix as he held out the torch.

Their journey after that was surprisingly uneventful.

As they drew closer to the summit, the plants and trees thinned, but they also didn't run into a single magic beast, as Yuui had feared. Those illguna were the first and the last.

Yuui looked at the burning wood in her hand and asked, "What is this thing?"

"It's made from esne."

"Esne. That's the one magic beasts dislike, right?"

"Yep. The smoke spreads out if you burn it as a torch. You can ward off magic beasts in a larger area like that. I bought it at a store in town."

"Then wouldn't it have been better just to use this from the start?"

"No, there wasn't any point."

"Huh?"

"I said you can ward off magic beasts with this, but to be honest, these esne torches aren't that effective. They help about as much as a good luck charm. Besides, there's no way you could ward off magic beasts that had gotten that close."

"But the illguna—"

"Yeah. Maybe the creatures on this mountain dislike esne way more than usual. Or maybe there's another reason... Anyway, I think the bonfires and torch meant something like this."

It took Yuui a moment to understand what Ix was talking about.

"No way... Are we re-creating the Dragon Remembrance?" she gasped.

Ix immediately acknowledged this absurd notion.

"Yep," he said.

"'Yep'...?"

"All festivals have their origins. I don't think the Eye of the Mountain, the Fulmeninia, was originally a pile of sand," explained Ix without turning back. "Is it normal to give a mound of debris as grand a name as that?"

"I don't know what you would consider normal."

"The ceremony that the festival originated from would have had 'the real thing.' If you say 'the mountain' to anyone in this town, they all think of the same place. There's a 'person of purity,' who heads to the summit but isn't allowed to receive help. There's also the Light in the Eye of the Mountain, the Sabineit Fulmeninia, which is the act of using a torch to light the dragon effigy. Don't you feel like they must represent something?"

"The Eye of the Mountain is Mount Agnas, the person of purity is the person who climbs the peak, and the Light in the Eye of the Mountain is the act of carrying a torch as you climb...?"

"It has to be. Or rather, I wish I could say for certain, but that's what seems most likely. Dragon Remembrance was a festival that reenacted climbing the mountain."

"How did you ever arrive at that connection?"

"At first, they probably actually climbed the peak. Then at some point, it was simplified and got replaced with a festival that took place in town. So it stands to reason that we just have to try re-creating the ceremony."

"And how exactly do we do that?"

"Yeah, that's the problem." Ix nodded. "The important part is the treasure you get from the dragon effigy..."

"So were there 'real' gold nuggets?"

"Mount Agnas isn't a gold mine. It wouldn't make sense for that to be the reward you get for scaling it. Unless that was actually—"

"If all of this was true, then what was the purpose of holding a ceremony or a festival? If there was that much to gain, what possible reason could they have for limiting it to a single person a year— Oh." Realization dawned on Yuui as she spoke. "It was so the priests could monopolize it. So that they could make a limited resource last for as long as possible. They restricted access to the summit and hid their secret behind the cover of the festival."

"Pessimistic assumption of you to make, but perhaps."

"But even if you think we should try re-creating it, we are not children. And it also isn't night."

"Those were probably details added later."

"What makes you think that?"

"No matter how low the elevation of this mountain is, no child could climb it alone. And an adult probably couldn't manage it at night, either. That leads me to believe those elements were tacked on to the ceremony afterward."

"...I suppose that could be true."

"The 'person of purity' label probably had less to do with them being a child and more to do with them being unable to recognize the truth despite the fact that they were participating in the ceremony. Someone who couldn't go around telling everyone what had transpired up there, in other words. It's possible the priests or their families did the ceremony as well..."

"That's an unpleasant thought."

Ix said nothing in response. Instead, he just held his hand out to ask for the torch.

They were nearing the summit and had moved into an area with piles of black stone.

The slope grew steeper, so they had to scramble up on both hands and feet. Yuui crouched on a boulder, gritting her teeth in pain as the straps from her bag dug into her shoulders.

When she looked over at Ix to see how he was doing, she found him nimbly climbing the incline. Was this the same shut-in who did nothing but craft wands? Where was he finding this stamina? Maybe he moved so dexterously since he didn't weigh much.

The air got thinner and thinner, and the smoke hanging in the area made breathing even more difficult. Tears streamed from her eyes, but she kept scrambling upward, coughing over and over. Now it seemed obvious to her why there was no one climbing this mountain—who would choose to travel to a place like this?

Banishing unrelated thoughts from her mind, Yuui instead focused entirely on getting over each rock in front of her. If the stone she grabbed on to seemed as if it would break off, she would have to search for a different route. And if she tumbled accidentally, she would plummet into the rocks below. That was the worst-case scenario. Now she was far more anxious than when they'd faced off against the illguna.

"Hey."

"...Huh?"

Yuui raised her head in response to the call and saw Ix holding his hand out toward her.

Nothing but sky stretched beyond him.

Gazing downward, she saw a long stretch of piled rocks.

"Take my hand," pleaded Ix.

"No... I'll climb...on my own!"

Yuui reached the summit without grabbing his hand.

The peak was a huge circular shape with massive boulders strewn about as far as the eye could see. The edge was probably the highest point of the mountain. It dipped down as you traveled toward its center, where the mouth of the volcano was probably located.

Yuui dropped her bag and sat by Ix's feet. She pulled off her stuffy, pointless coat. Took several ragged breaths. Swung her arms gently and waited for the numbness to fade.

"It's a beautiful view," she said in admiration.

"Mm."

From the mountain's zenith, everything at the base looked hazy. There was Agnasruze, with its plain, quiet rows of buildings. The road leaving town was brown, and the crops in the fields swayed in the wind. If she strained her eyes, she could make out a red spot close to Agnasruze. She'd seen the halni field from all the way up here.

Once they'd finished resting, they circled around the summit, taking care not to fall. To the northeast, they could see the mountain range continue far off into the distance. Those mountains were even taller than this one.

After one lap around, they headed toward the crater of the volcano.

As they closed in, the ground suddenly gave way and opened into a deep hole with cliff-like sides.

An unending stream of white smoke puffed out of the opening, bringing with it a strange smell. Yuui checked the cloth over her mouth and wondered if she was okay to breathe it in.

Due to the angle of the sun, its rays didn't reach the bottom of the hole, which was cloaked in an impenetrable darkness. All they knew was that it was quite deep.

"There's no pool of lava?" murmured Yuui. She'd wondered

if there was going to be a boiling pool of lava, but she'd never climbed a volcano before, so she wouldn't know.

She looked up at Ix next to her and asked, "...Right, what now?"

"Hmm... There wasn't any other ceremony in the festival beyond what we've done." He furrowed his brow. "Like, you'd just climb the mountain, and then there'd be treasure lying around."

"Do we have any other clues? If we do what the Dragon Remembrance did, then we...burn an effigy?"

"Burn... What is there to burn?"

Instead of gold nuggets and treasure scattered about, there was nothing but black stone. There were no signs of vegetation.

"Perhaps...," Yuui said, looking around the summit, "...when they actually climbed the mountain, there was something. Maybe dragon hearts flew out during an eruption and fell to the rocky earth. Someone took those and bragged about stealing them from a dragon."

She cast her eyes down and thought back.

"But as time passed, they didn't find more dragon hearts. Most likely because of a reduction in large eruptions. However, the priest would look bad if they came away with nothing. To rectify this, they changed the treasure into gold nuggets, made the festival finish off within the town's limits, and somehow managed to maintain the faith...until they gave the town up to the New Order."

"So we're too late?"

"It's just a thought." Yuui shrugged.

"...Right."

Ix's expressions might not change much, but he certainly wasn't expressionless. Yuui had come to realize this after spending as much time with him as she had. Even so, this was the most morose she'd ever seen him. He looked almost like a child who'd been scolded as he shrank back.

"It was a foolhardy quest from the beginning, Ix. We started with not a single lead, then made theory upon theory until we finally arrived here. That was one success, at least. I'm grateful you have given your all to this," Yuui consoled him.

"Don't bother trying to make me feel better."

"I was only—"

"It's fine. Just means I really am half a craftsman in the end." Ix hung his head. "*Haah...* I should have let Morna take care of it, or..."

Yuui cleared her throat and said, "Well, this isn't the end just yet."

"...What do you mean?"

He turned to her in utter confusion and absolute seriousness, which made Yuui smile.

"Even if we cannot manage a dragon heart, I still need my wand fixed. Would you help me with that, Ix?"

"Hmm... Guess I could borrow Morna's shop again."

"I have to go rescue those three. And summer will be over soon. We need to make it in time for the start of next semester at the Academy."

"You're right... We have to hurry back."

"Yes, exactly."

In contrast with what he'd just said, though, Ix made no move to go back. He stayed rooted to the spot, his head turned downward the whole time.

"Um, Ix?" Yuui looked up at his profile. "Are you all right? I know you're upset, but we—"

"Can I try one last thing?" asked Ix as he hung his head. No, not as he hung his head—as he peered into the crater.

"Hmm? What is it?"

"Just a hunch."

"What?" Yuui thought hard. "I don't really get it, but do as you like."

"'Kay."

Ix held up the torch and threw it into the crater.

It skipped down the slope, tumbled toward the bottom of the hole, and disappeared into the darkness.

Atop the mountain, they heard nothing more than the wind.

They waited awhile. Eventually, Yuui tried to keep her tone gentle as she asked, "And what was that for?"

"Looks like it didn't work." Ix sighed. "Tried 'lighting the effigy' in my own way. Was that bad?"

"You thought dragon hearts would fly out if you threw the torch into the volcano's crater? I see—what a pleasant idea."

"……"

"Regardless of the correctness of your hunch, however… Um, now that you've thrown away our torch, how are we going to get back?"

"The smell is probably on our clothes from when we ascended, and the magic beasts here are fairly tame, all things considered. I think we'll be fine," Ix answered calmly.

"Huh…all right. Then let's pray that at least your final theory is correct." Yuui put her coat back on. "Shall we go?"

"Yeah."

The last thing they did before leaving was to peer down into the volcano's mouth.

White smoke leaked from the tranquil darkness.

That was all.

They nodded slightly and turned away.

And only managed a few more steps.

"What the?" cried Yuui as she stopped dead in her tracks, dumbstruck.

She glanced at Ix; he wore a similar expression.

"Yuui, be careful!"

"Be careful? How?!"

"I don't know—!"

Ix's voice was quickly drowned out.

Something roared so loudly that no voice could compete with it.

No human could make that sound.

Nor could any magic beast.

Nor any living creature.

It was Mount Agnas.

The mountain was roaring.

5

The explosive sound surging up from deep underground made Ix's ears ring.

Then the air moved quickly enough to become a concussive force, sending stones and even boulders lurching.

"Shit!"

Ix instantly reached out to Yuui. They clung to each other, trying to regain their footing.

"Does this mean it's going to erupt?!" she shouted.

"All because of the torch I threw in?!" he shouted back.

"If it is, I'll hate you for the rest of my life!"

"There's not much of your life left, so use it for something better!"

As they yelled back and forth, the roar faded little by little, and the tremors also diminished.

Finally, the sound completely stopped, and silence returned. The stark change in volume filled Ix's ears with a high-pitched ringing.

Yuui lowered her arms and murmured, "It subsided?"

"I don't know. Let's get out of here before a second wave hits."

"Agreed..."

Just as they started to move away from the crater, they heard another sound.

"Huh...?"

They stopped and turned back.

©Enji

It wasn't the loud roar from before but a low, gentle rumble.
No... It wasn't a sound.
It was a voice.

"Long has it been, people of fire."

"Wh-what was that...?" yelped Yuui as she looked around, searching for the source of the voice. But she found no one other than Ix, of course.

"No, Yuui. It's not up here."

"B-but then where...?"

"There," he said, pointing into the crater. "The voice came from there."

"From the bottom of the crater...?"

"No...not from the bottom of a 'crater.'"

Ix brought his hand to his mouth and shook his head. He realized his hands were quivering. He'd had so many "theories" since he'd accepted this request. Ix hadn't even told Yuui about the most unrealistic, fanciful hypothesis he'd had. But now it was coming true.

"What does that mean, Ix?!" shouted Yuui.

"It's a dragon."

"What?"

"What we're standing on right now isn't a mountain... It's a dragon. Agnas isn't the name of a volcano—it's the name of a *dragon*," asserted Ix. He took a few unsteady steps and shouted, "Am I right?!"

"...You are indeed," confirmed the voice.

This time they could hear it clearly. It was a deep, calm voice, but it spoke gently to them.

"We are what you call a dragon, we are what you call Agnas, we are what you call Fulmeninia, and we are what you call a mountain."

"The mountain…is a dragon?" Yuui shook her head over and over in disbelief.

"…I was about to say it before," said Ix, almost to himself. "Yuui, you posited dragons were still alive but hadn't been seen in a while because they had shrunk or turned invisible. That last hypothesis struck me. Just like if they became so small you couldn't see them, what if dragons had grown so large as to be nearly invisible?"

The agnasite veins never ran out. Fragments of agnasite poured from the fissures in the abandoned mine.

Ix had thought dragon heart, some sort of strange gemstone, had produced those lesser gems… But there was a far more natural explanation than a stone creating a stone.

Put simply…

…the dragon heart was a heart.

It sent something throughout the mountain, the dragon's body.

Whatever circulated throughout its massive form crystallized when it bled out.

"It wasn't a coincidence that the compound core made of shinee aletts and agnasite was similar to the dragon heart. Of course they would be similar—they're both partway between a mineral and a living tissue. That strong thumping I felt before wasn't just in my mind…"

Even though he was the one saying this, Ix also couldn't believe it. Not even fairy tales would depict a mountain who was a dragon. Who would believe such a childish fantasy…?

"…I have awaited your arrival. When last did you come…?" Agnas inquired, slowly stringing the words together.

"Th-there aren't any records of dragons in the past thousand years," Ix stuttered.

"A thousand years… We understand little of the calendar used by the people of fire… But that would seem to be quite some time."

"Y-you understand our language?" asked Yuui, also quite frightened.

"Yes, we do." The air rumbled every time Agnas spoke. "Our eyes see to the horizon, and our ears hear every feather that glances off the water's surface. If we wish to speak with you, we can even know your hearts, regardless of the distance."

"Dragon magic...," murmured Ix.

Dragons had unlimited magic and could create anything they could imagine, so what Agnas was describing shouldn't have been a surprise.

Ix felt as if his knees were on the verge of giving out, but he resisted sinking to the ground and said, "You told us we came before. What kind of people were they? Do you remember?"

"We are unable to tell apart you people of fire... Yet, yes, they only ever came alone. Though, at that time, we were smaller than we are now."

"W-wait," interjected Yuui. "You were smaller? I've never seen a record indicating Mount Agnas was smaller. Why did you get bigger? Just how long ago are we talking?"

Her shout echoed across the summit.

There was a pause afterward, and the mountain started trembling. They were hit with small, quick vibrations accompanied by a strange noise.

Agnas was laughing.

"...I see now. You know not of us," it chuckled with some amusement.

"There are a number of legends, but...," started Ix. "I at least have never met someone who's seen a dragon."

"I see, I see."

"Um, Agnas, would you please tell me something? Why are you here? What did you mean when you said you became bigger?"

"As you wish."

Agnas quickly agreed to her request, but Ix still couldn't wrap his head around the situation. To a dragon, humans would be nothing more than insects crawling across its skin. So why was it being so kind to them? Ix suddenly imagined an old beast who'd calmly accepted its death.

"Are you certain, though? We have the time, but you people of fire are given so little of it," warned Agnas.

"Well, if you could just give us a brief overview," said Ix, to which the dragon laughed again.

"How amusing... The other people of fire who came here did not converse as you two do."

"I-I'm sorry, have we offended you...?" asked Yuui.

"No, no, all is as it should be. That is why I am here."

And so, Agnas began its story.

"Not even I know from whence we came. I am the last of our generation. When my eyes first opened, we soared through the skies, and we made our homes in the forests and mountains—in distant jungles, dark woodlands, great crags, mountain chains, and this very rock here."

"In the forests and mountains...?" murmured Yuui.

"Yes. At the time, we were not so large as we are now. We had a relationship with you people of fire, and we granted you what you desired. And how different the things you lusted after were. At times, it was gold; at others, knowledge or life—I have even granted swords and the like."

That sounded almost like the kind of treasure a hero got when killing a dragon or when a priestess beseeched a dragon.

"Wait a second," interrupted Ix as he held a hand up. "You gave them what they wanted? What do you get out of that? Even helping humans—"

"It is not only the people of fire whom we assist. We fulfill the wishes of other peoples as well."

"O-other peoples?"

"The people of black wings, the people of blue scales, and the people of twisted horns, which you two met before. There are many other peoples besides our own, and we draw on the energy they release. We give them what they covet so that we may return the favor. Though you, the people of fire, were the first to come to us wanting something other than sustenance, the first to come and speak with us..."

"You draw energy... Is that the source of your power?" asked Ix.

He and Yuui had discussed this before: Where would dragons get the energy to sustain their infinite magic and massive bodies? If they had the ability to absorb the magic that living creatures gave off, then you could truly call that infinite. As long as it didn't have a cap...

"You people of fire were intriguing. There were those of you who actively engaged with us, while there were others who attempted to sever their connection with us. It was particularly amusing to interact with you through the medium of language. There were those among you who spoke of many things. That was the first joy I knew. And yet..."

Agnas's words ceased for an instant, and white smoke blew from the crater.

"...an eternity had passed since we began. Many of us were tired. At one point, one of our kind decided to sleep and become one with the earth. When they did, others wished for that same respite. However, one of you people of fire happened to learn of our coming slumber and made a request. Said they, 'We will be lost without you. Would you find a way to continue trading with us?' Thus, we selected one of our youngest and tasked them with all future interactions."

"And that was you, Agnas?" inquired Ix.

"It was indeed. That person of fire was unusual. We agreed upon a signal to be used at each visit, and we promised we would not speak outside of those times. Their kind always came one at a time. In accordance with their wish, I oversaw all engagements. The others of my kind were relieved. They drifted to sleep on top of me, one after another. Our bodies combined, and I became we.

Even those of my generation eventually tired of life and sank into a torpor. And then we became longer and larger still."

In other words...

...it wasn't just Mount Agnas. The entire mountain range that stretched far to the northeast was a dragon collective?

"I know not how long ago that was on your calendar. That is the answer to your question."

"Are you not...?" started Yuui. "Are you not tired?"

"I will not tire, so long as the people of fire come. I was chosen because I find a particular joy in our interactions. However..." Smoke billowed from the crater again. "From some point onward, you no longer came. We no longer engaged in conversation; you only wished from the foothills. And even that came to an end. There are a small few who come this way and a number who dig into my body, but they give no signal, nor do they wish for anything. A very few have reached these heights since, only to go far away. I simply continue to wait. I gather the carved material from inside my body and spew it from my mouth. Sometimes I doze. Yes, since this has become the norm...I suppose I have become weary."

The records stated that dragons went extinct over a thousand years ago.

At some point, interactions with Agnas had morphed into town festivals, and now even that had gone.

How long had Agnas been biding its time?

It had become an immobile mountain. It had endured years upon years of waiting with no end in sight.

"Why?" Ix couldn't stop the word slipping from his lips.

"What do you ask?"

"Why...do you still continue to do the task you were assigned? I get that the other dragons entrusted it to you, but you've done plenty. You're tired but refuse sleep, even though humans don't visit you. No one would even notice if you went back on your word now. What reason do you have to keep waiting here by your lonesome? To keep doing what a bunch of people who aren't here anymore told you to...?"

"Ah," said Agnas gently. "So long as I have what I was entrusted with, then I am we, person of fire. I am never truly alone."

"...Oh, I guess so." Ix shook his head a few times, then slowly spoke again. "Agnas...the steps to interact with dragons, that signal included, haven't been passed down. Nobody knows that you exist, that you dwell here."

"I see... I had suspected as much."

A strong wind blew away the smoke.

"Yet, you have remembered. People of fire, you have not forgotten me. You came here and gave the signal and conversed with me. If you have, might not others as well? Might they not visit me, as they did in the past? Is that not possible?"

"...It's not, Agnas."

"Ix!" Yuui glared at him.

"I'm just speaking the truth. We made it here essentially by accident. I don't think others can do the same."

"We just need to spread the word!"

"We don't have that kind of power," Ix countered firmly. "So we might be able to spread the word to the few people who are near us. But who'd believe us? And even if someone does, that kind of knowledge is fragile. In the grand scheme of things, we're going to die soon, and anyone we tell would die soon. That's why the people made a festival so long ago; they knew people would forget eventually. That way, the story would be passed down to future generations and internalized, even if they would forget most of the details... But as strong a method of passing on information as it was, the festival was still lost. And now, those who only barely remember it are going to disappear soon..."

Ix shut his mouth.

"...I see," murmured Agnas. "You will no longer come."

"Agnas, I will—," started Yuui.

"No... It is fine, person of fire."

Smoke rose again from the mountaintop.

The distant view faded as white fog settled in.

"So if that is the shape of things, then my task has been fulfilled. The wants of the people of fire have been fulfilled...and perhaps that is fine. I will slumber, and we shall bring a brief chapter of history to a close."

"But that's...," started Yuui. Her shoulders sagged. "It's like a chapter of a book that no one ever read or was even aware of, so it simply rotted away..."

"What're you talking about?" asked Ix.

"No, it's nothing..." She smiled quietly. "Are there no other dragons awake besides you?"

"There are not. I am the last."

"......"

Agnas's gentle voice came from the direction of the white smoke.

"Tell me your desire. No matter your wish, I shall grant it."

Ix and Yuui exchanged glances.

They nodded to each other, and Ix raised his hands.

"I wish for your...for a dragon heart. About as big as I can carry is fine," he stated.

"Understood. So you shall have."

"I-is that okay?" Yuui couldn't help but ask. "It's your heart..."

"There are a number of hearts within my body," replied Agnas. "If there were not, they could not carry the warmth throughout its entirety. Losing one or two is simply a fragment of the whole, so it will do no harm. Here."

From the center of the smoke rose a gemstone so large, you could wrap your arms around it.

It was red. Steaming. Something between a mineral and the flesh of a living creature.

It was a dragon heart.

"There was one other before who also asked for one of my hearts...," noted Agnas.

It floated to Ix and settled in his arms, weighing them down.
"It's heavy! And hot!" he shrieked.

Ix nearly tossed it aside but somehow managed to hold on to it without letting it go.

He looked at the glimmering red object in his arms. He felt as if he could hear a faint *thump, thump.*

He finally had it.

As he gazed at the dragon heart, a grin spread across his face. With this much, he could craft wands to his heart's content.

"Now, tell me your other wish," said Agnas.

"...Huh?" said Yuui. "I—I thought...it was only one wish?"

"There has never been such a restriction. There are two of you. Therefore, I shall fulfill two wishes. Speak, person of fire."

"I-Ix...," stammered Yuui as she looked at Ix with unease.

"Ask for what you want, Yuui," he insisted.

"But the dragon heart is for me!"

"No. What you wanted was for the wand to be mended. Needing a dragon heart for it was merely something for myself."

They were each reflected in the other's eyes.

Eventually, Yuui nodded.

"...All right." She wetted her parched lips. "Agnas...are there people inside you?"

"Yes, there are many."

"Um, not those ones. I mean, any within your body who are trapped? There should be three of them."

"Hmm... I am not certain if they are unable to leave, but some have not moved in quite a while. But there are indeed three. They are caught partway down one of my vessels."

"Are they...s-still alive?"

"They are. It is weak, but the flame of life still burns within them. All three of them."

"Oh, thank goodness..." Yuui let out a sigh of relief. "Agnas, please, please rescue those three!"

"Is that what you wish?"

"…Yes."

"Understood. So shall you receive."

"Th-thank you!" She bowed.

"No…it is I who should thank you."

The smoke slowly cleared.

It vanished to reveal a clear blue sky.

"I would thank both of you, people of fire, for remembering me, for journeying here."

"N-no, thank you so much. I pray from the bottom of my heart that your slumber is peaceful," said Yuui.

"Slumber is, by its nature, a peaceful thing. But your kindness brings me joy."

"…I-Ix, don't you want to say something?"

"Hmm? Oh, yeah." He seemed unsure of what to say until Yuui prodded him. Then, suddenly, he began with, "…Hey, Agnas."

"Yes?"

"Do dragons also become dust when they go to sleep?"

The mountain momentarily shook in delight.

And then the voice of the last dragon came no more.

Yuui and Ix lingered on a mountaintop scene that was just as it had been when they'd arrived.

6

Yuui and Ix descended the mountain.

They climbed down the rocks, passed through the under-brush they had cut away, and marched down the forest trail.

No magic beasts appeared on their trip back.

"By the way…," Yuui said to Ix as they walked. "Was Agnas's answer helpful?"

"What answer?"

"Why it still did what people who were gone had told it to."

"Oh...no, that wasn't really what I meant by my question." Ix looked upward slightly.

Perhaps Agnas had realized the question had been intended for Ix himself.

And Ix had understood that as he'd listened to Agnas's answer.

The sadness he'd felt as he left the shop back then—it wasn't sentimental attachment to the home he'd grown up in...

Ix sighed, hiding his emotions from Yuui.

And so his reason had been the same as Agnas's.

As long as he had something that had been entrusted to him, then the dead were not truly gone.

That contract had filled the hole left by his master's death.

But Ix wouldn't share that with anyone.

He sealed his reasoning deep within his heart and did not think of it again.

It was too painful to acknowledge.

He felt like a child.

"By the way, why did the townsfolk make that agreement with the dragon?" Yuui wondered aloud, changing the subject as if she'd been deliberating over it. "Whatever you wished for, the dragon would grant you. And yet, they limited it to only a single request from a single individual a year..."

"You're the one who said it was probably so the priests could monopolize on the profit, aren't you?"

"Well, yes. But..." Yuui brought a hand to her mouth. "What about this? If something could conveniently grant everything you could imagine, then people would overuse it. Perhaps they were trying to protect the dragon from humans by hiding it behind a ceremony..."

"That would be ironic, considering it was because they hid it behind a ceremony that people forgot the original intent and stopped climbing the mountain."

"Agnas is too kind. It even granted the wishes of people who didn't climb the mountain..." Yuui sighed. "We've researched so much, yet there are so many riddles still left. For instance, how *did* the New Order so completely eliminate the old faith?"

"We've gone over it before." Ix nodded slightly. "Because the townspeople were angry that the priests hoarded all the treasure from the festival."

"But the opposite is also possible. If they actually took that treasure and spread it throughout town, then the people would get rich. They all happily held their faith, and so the New Order had to come down hard."

There was a loud flapping of wings, and a black bird flew over their heads. It quickly disappeared behind the tree branches.

"Documents... If we search, we might find records about that," posited Yuui.

"We're out of time. We couldn't find out why."

"*Sigh...* There's so much we don't understand."

"That's normal."

The only thing that spoke of the past were records.

So they would learn nothing else of this place.

How lively was that lost festival?

How kind was the dragon they had sung of?

No document could tell them that.

7

When Ix opened his eyes, a ray from the morning sun peeked into the room. He rubbed his eyes and sat up. He moved Morna, who was sleeping on the pile on top of him. She let out a groan when she hit the ground.

Ix yawned and went to the front of the shop.

Excited by the opportunity to work with the dragon heart, he and Morna had stirred themselves into a frenzy. For the past few days, they'd labored until their bodies couldn't, sleeping only when they passed out from exhaustion.

When Ix entered the hallway, Yuui turned to him.

With her hands on her hips, she said, "Good morning. It's already noon."

"Mm, morning."

"It's not good for you to go without rest—you know that, right?"

"My body will tell me its limits."

"Really..."

Ottou was there but didn't look toward Ix. He was engrossed with cleaning the shop. With his small grin plastered perpetually on his face, he took the scattered materials and furniture and put them back in their place.

Ix sat in a chair and bit into a hunk of bread.

The wand repair was going well, since he also had Morna's help. It seemed they might just be able to finish it in time for Yuui's next semester.

"Anyway, please stop pushing yourself so much," insisted Yuui as she pulled her hood far down over her face.

"You going out?" asked Ix.

"Yes, I have a promise to—"

Just as she was about to open the door to leave, someone opened it from the other side.

"Hello!" came the high-pitched voice.

A young girl stood in the entrance. She had long golden hair and wore high-end clothing, though her outfit was slightly over-size. It appeared that a daughter of a noble family had somehow wandered into their filthy hole-in-the-wall.

She beamed a smile as bright as the sun and looked at each of the three people in the shop in turn.

"Shigan Aym," said Ottou immediately.

She spoke again before Ix could ask how Ottou knew her.

"You figured me out even like this... Interesting." The girl brought a hand to her chin. "We should assume my appearance didn't tip you off. Perhaps my posture or my accent allowed you to determine my identity..."

Ix was surprised by the sudden change in the girl's tone, and then she quickly began to expand.

There was an odd popping sound as each of the bones in her body warped.

Then an old man stood before them.

He was quite tall and of bony build, but he had perfectly straight posture. He resembled a narrow beam. The wrinkles cut deep into his face, and his eyes glinted like a hawk's. His white hair was cut short.

Standing next to him was Yuui, who suddenly had to look up at him.

"Uh...P-Professor Shigan?" she asked.

"Hmm? Are you a student at the Academy?" Shigan raised an eyebrow.

"Y-y-yes... My name is Yuui Laika."

"Yuui... The study abroad student from Lukutta. Have you come for a wand order as well?"

"No, I have requested a wand repair..."

"I see. Ms. Morna's skills are top class. To excel at magic, you must first find an excellent wandmaker. You have quite the potential."

"Th-thank you."

"Are you a student as well?" Shigan turned his eyes toward Ix.

"No." His denial was blunt.

"Oh, h-he's a wandmaker as well," clarified Yuui hurriedly. "His name is Ix. He's actually the one I asked to repair my wand."

"Ah...Munzil's last apprentice?"

"...Yeah," answered Ix.

"Ix, you're being rude!"

"No, it's no problem. Wandmakers place wands above people.

As they should," said Shigan before turning to look down at Yuui. "Anyhow, were you about to leave?"

"Oh, yes, I was, but..."

"Pay me no mind, then. Feel free to go. We shall meet again at the Academy."

"Y-yes, sir." Yuui looked between Shigan and Ix and vaguely bowed her head. "I-I'll be taking my leave, then..."

As that was happening, Ottou had brought a staff over from the rack in the shop. It was painted completely white, with a blue gem embedded in the top.

"Here it is," said Ottou as he handed it over to the professor.

"Mm, thank you, Ottou."

He took the staff and slipped it into his inside pocket. It disappeared from sight, though there was no way it could have fit.

His eyes swept the shop until they came to settle on Ix again.

"Ix, would you mind taking a walk with me?" he asked.

"Huh?"

"I have something to speak with you about. Come with me." Shigan opened the shop door as if it was a given that the other person would do as he ordered. "Ottou, please express my thanks to Ms. Morna."

"Okay." Ottou nodded.

Shigan tucked his chin in slightly, then turned and left.

Not knowing what else to do, Ix also left the store. Shigan was apparently a fast walker, as he'd already moved some distance down the street.

Ix jogged to catch up and fell in beside him.

The sounds from the busy main street drifted to where they were.

"Munzil did a lot for me," noted Shigan with no other introduction. "Many of the wands and staffs I own were crafted by his hands. He was the greatest wandmaker in history. His death was a terrible loss for the magic community."

"Uh-huh."

"However, instead of wands, he left behind excellent apprentices, Ms. Morna being at the top of that list. I have already availed myself of her services on several occasions. The staff I received this time is also of superb craftsmanship."

"Morna would be happy to hear it."

"I will order from you in time as well."

"No point. I'm just half a craftsman."

"Is that so?"

Something suddenly struck Shigan.

There was a large brown stain on his clothes. Ix looked down the street to see a group of poor children who seemed to have hurled a ball of mud at him. They noticed Ix glaring at them and fled as quickly as possible.

But Shigan's eyebrows didn't even budge. He kept walking at the same pace, staring ahead as before. The complete lack of reaction made Ix wonder if he'd even noticed the mud ball.

Ix caught up with him again, and the professor said, "I met you once before. Do you remember?"

"No."

"Really? It was you who gave me the wand."

"I gave it to you?" Ix's brow crinkled for a while; then he murmured quietly, "...Engraved number 9889, Transmitted?"

"Ah, there's that memory. It was excellent even back then. I went to pick up the wand I had ordered, and Munzil called you over, just a little child. All he said was 'Get the wand.' An absurd order. Yet, in no time flat, you found the wand and brought it out from that horrifically cluttered shop."

"It's not that big a deal," countered Ix, frowning. "It might have looked cluttered, but it was organized. Everything was sorted how Master liked it, by crafted date, core material, wood material, disposition, engraved number. It was easy as long as you knew that."

"But for a child so young he could barely speak to have that kind of memory?"

"I was an abandoned kid. Anyone could do that if it ensured their survival."

Shigan nodded, then said, "This is a conversation we couldn't have had while Munzil was alive, but... He often talked about who among his apprentices had the most talent. He told me it was his last apprentice... That it was you, Ix."

"...That's ridiculous."

"No, it's true."

"Impossible. I don't have magic. I can't even use test magic. Even if I go through all the effort of making a wand, I can't test its abilities myself. Talent isn't even part of the equation—I've been half-baked from birth."

"It was *because* of that that you were peerless. Your greatest talent is the fact that you are unable to use magic."

"What are you saying?"

"Listen, if you wish to push a wand to its utmost potential, you have to see it from the outside. You can't go inside. Imagine if you were inside the belly of a massive beast. All you could see from in there would be the inside of its stomach. What you could understand would be only a fraction of the whole. You don't even know what the beast looks like, do you? It's the same for all kinds of things. If you look at something from the inside, all you can glimpse is a tiny portion of it. If you go outside, you can finally grasp its true nature. Using magic means you are trapped within its stomach. Once that happens, it doesn't matter how much you improve your skill—you will never be able to escape that viewpoint. In that regard, you are unblemished. Because you cannot use magic, you, and you alone, can observe it from the outside. You have a talent that no one else does."

"Who would say—?"

"Those were Munzil's words."

"Master...?"

The two continued, walking away from the main road.

The hubbub died down, and they finally returned to a quiet alley.

"I don't believe you. I don't have that kind of talent," Ix said.

"Hmm, you really think so?"

"Of course. What can I even do?" Ix glared at Shigan as if challenging him. "It's because I'm untalented that—"

"You fixed Ms. Yuui's wand, did you not? *That* wand." Shigan's eyes showed a brief sparkle. "Could any craftsman besides you have accomplished that?"

Ix suddenly came to a halt.

Shigan didn't seem to notice, and the sound of his footsteps grew distant.

"Shigan, you know about that wand...?" asked Ix.

The professor gave no reply.

Ix looked down the road, but there was no sign of Shigan.

Ix continued on, alone.

Shigan's words swirled through his mind.

Master?

Really?

He'd actually said that?

To look from the outside, not the inside?

"Ah... For the love of... It's this kind of thing," Ix muttered to himself, a hand to his forehead. "It's way too late for advice now..."

8

Curiosity was plastered on all the faces of the people gathered on the main street.

They were staring at the Lukutta delegation in the middle of the road where a group of people walked—their skin brown, their hair black, and their clothing unfamiliar.

They were likely treated as some sort of strange exhibition

when they'd arrived in the capital as well. It seemed they drew quite the crowd. Yuui sighed.

A person in the mob would cheer, then another would jeer, and then it would devolve into a huge ruckus. You couldn't tell if they were taunting the delegation or welcoming them. All Yuui knew was that if her hood hadn't been on, she would have been treated exactly the same.

Separated from the crowd, Yuui stood facing another person.

"...How have you been feeling afterward?" she asked.

"Ah, no problems. Dann and Rozalia seem good, too. That all happened, but it's so weird...," said Tomah with a bewildered smile. "Actually, I say 'That all happened,' but I don't even know what 'that' is. We broke the wall in the abandoned mine and fell into a river, and it's blank after that."

"I'm just glad you're not hurt."

"...But really, what was that?"

By the time they'd come to, Tomah, Dann, and Rozalia were collapsed on the sand mound in Agnasruze for some reason. It caused an uproar, since there was the question of how a group who had supposedly met an unfortunate end had gotten there, but there had been other reasons for the commotion.

For one, despite the square's heavy foot traffic, not a single person saw the moment they arrived. It wasn't as if they fell from the sky or came up from the ground. They just appeared in an instant, as though they'd been there from the beginning.

Another strange thing was that they had all been coated in blood, from head to toe. They'd been dyed completely red, worse than you would even expect from a mangled corpse. Yet, there also hadn't been a single identifiable wound on their bodies. They'd undergone harsh interrogation about whose blood it belonged to.

In the end, with some help from Tomah's family, they'd returned to Leirest without incident, though the questions only grew from there. Even Yuui wasn't sure how they'd gone uninjured.

Either they'd been unbelievably lucky or someone had wished for their safety, and their wish had been fulfilled.

"...Anyway, Yuui. Thanks for taking the time to talk," said Tomah.

"I did promise."

"Then let me just get this out," prefaced Tomah, sobering up. "I'm sorry for the insensitive things I said back then. It was my fault. So...why don't you come and be an adventurer with us again? I know I've hurt you, and if there's anything I can do to fix it, I will. I know I'm being selfish, but please. We need you."

"Aren't you being a little too flattering?" chided Yuui gently. "Is this proposal meant for my own good?"

"Yeah, well, I won't deny that I've got a selfish desire to help you, but I meant what I said. You are excellent both in your studies and in magic. I have no idea how many times you've saved our bacon. So...please, will you help us?"

"...Tomah, thank you."

"So—" Tomah's expression brightened.

"But I'm sorry—I cannot accept," Yuui admitted, holding up a hand. "I am grateful for everything you three have done for me since I arrived at the Academy. You treated me with such kindness, even though I came from an enemy country and could barely speak your language. Truly...I couldn't repay you even if I worked for my entire life to make it up."

She paused and shook her head.

"But I can't be with you. For the sake of our happiness," she said.

"I know I—"

"Please don't misunderstand. Tomah, I don't hate you. And I don't hate your father. This won't change the fact that we will still be classmates. The person I hated..."

She looked down and touched her earring.

"...To be honest," she mumbled, her voice low, "I planned on getting revenge."

"Huh? O-on whom?" yelped Tomah in a panic, and he looked left and right.

"It was...," started Yuui, and she smiled sadly.

It was before the wand broke.

She spoke with Tomah at the Academy, and she felt despair.

She despaired at her own stupidity.

The one she'd thought foolish was herself.

And then the delegation... How they, like her past self, so optimistically believed they could come to understand one another if they talked.

Yuui had wanted to show them how foolish that sentiment was. And to do that, she would show them her revenge.

She would exact vengeance.

On whom?

On the liar.

The liar who'd told her he had no desire to die yet never came back.

She would get revenge with the wand he'd placed in her hand.

He told her to live, and so she would get her revenge.

She did it as soon as she thought of it.

Brought the wand to her own throat.

Closed her eyes.

Then there had been a shattering sound.

But she knew now that the liar hadn't lied. She'd realized it when she'd glimpsed that wandmaker apprentice's face.

"It was...an immoral thing. I can no longer do immoral things," admitted Yuui.

"I don't really understand..." Tomah crossed his arms. "Yuui, you're not the kind of person who can do something immoral."

"So it seems to you."

Yuui adjusted her hood so it wouldn't be blown off by the wind.

Then she looked straight forward and stared at Tomah.

"Tomah, we cannot come to understand each other. Just as

there are some things you can never grasp no matter how much you research, no matter how much we talk things over, we are two people who cannot empathize with each other. That is why we can't be together. We can chat at school, and we can learn side by side. But…it's still impossible for us to be together right now. Neither of us did anything wrong; it is just a simple fact. We're never going to see eye to eye."

"But, Yuui!" shouted Tomah. "You said 'right now,' yeah? Does that mean I can hope we will understand each other someday?"

The crowd grew louder.

If that was to happen, she thought.

If that was to happen, it would be far in the future.

Once the beginning had been forgotten and only a festival remained.

When they weren't just two countries, allied in name only but connected by true discourse.

On the day when the delegation from the east could walk down this street and meet a joyous welcome.

Even someone who'd refused to speak to anyone, just to uphold an agreement, had gotten their wish granted after many years.

"Yes. Yes, you can," said Yuui. She had a truly happy smile on her face. "It may be a hundred years from now, or maybe a thousand, but someday we will."

Yuui waited for the stagecoach to depart. The station reeked of beasts and feces. A dry wind blew through and whipped up a cloud of dust.

Beside her stood Ix. He'd come to see her off. He'd turned into quite the customer pleaser, compared with how he was when they first met.

Ix had decided to stay at Morna's shop for the time being as an apprentice. The majority of the money they'd made selling the enedo teeth had disappeared into their dragon heart research. Even so, Morna's shop didn't have that much leeway in terms of finances, so they would certainly be unable to host him soon. When that time came, he planned on using his connections with the other apprentices of Munzil to travel from region to region by joining their shops. Depending on the scale of their operations, he could even be granted his craftsman license. He complained that it would be forever before he had his own shop.

They sat in silence for a while, until Yuui suddenly said, "Something has been on my mind."

"What's that?" asked Ix with a tilt of his head.

"The request form you found in the Adventurers' Guild storage. The one on black slate. What was that?"

"That...? Who knows." Ix shrugged, then spread his hands. "It was from a long time ago. The request probably came from someone who misunderstood the festival."

"Can I tell you what I think?"

"What's that?"

Yuui adjusted her seat and cleared her throat.

"It was a request from Munzil."

"...What?"

"When he made this wand, he realized the connection between the dragon heart and agnasite. He thought there were clues to dragons in Mount Agnas. With that in mind, he went to the Guild and put in a request. Obviously, he didn't think it would be fulfilled. He had an ulterior motive for submitting it. Do you know what that was?"

Ix stared at Yuui, dumbstruck.

"It was to leave a clue for his apprentice. He knew a time would come when his apprentice would need a dragon heart, so he carved a request on stone, which is sturdy, degrades little, and would stand out from the others above all else. If the Guild stored his request in accordance with their regulations, it would remain long after he had expired."

"Th-that's just a theory—"

"Furthermore," continued Yuui, "your master may also have realized the mountain itself was the dragon."

"H-how could you say that?" Ix's voice trembled.

"Do you remember the characters on the request form? You thought it was written in old-fashioned grammar with no prepositions, but what if it was something that should have been written without them? In other words, it wasn't meant to be 'Research Dragon *in* Mount Agnas'; it was meant to be 'Research *Dragon Mount Agnas.*'"

Ix went quiet for a while, then eventually shook his head.

"No...that's impossible. I can maybe accept the idea that he made the request. I'll even go out on a limb and say, for the sake of argument, that he noticed the relationship between the dragon heart and agnasite. But...for him to figure out the true nature of the dragon with only those few clues... No human could manage that. And he was human. Or at least I thought he was..."

"Well, I suppose." Yuui was satisfied to see Ix looking more frightened than ever. "Forget about it. It was just a flight of fancy."

She felt the wand in her inside pocket. The core had been swapped out, and its performance surpassed even its previous iteration. The memory of how she'd given it a quick test wave, then accidentally started a small fire because she'd miscalculated how much she should have held back, was still fresh in her mind.

The coach driver stood in front of the waiting area, gave a big wave, and shouted that the next car was leaving soon. That was the one Yuui would be taking.

Casually, she told Ix, "Try not to die."

"What?" Ix said, his eyebrows knit.

"Don't fail to handle a wand properly and go dying on me."

"Dying isn't on my to-do list."

"Yes. Thank you."

"What are you talking about?"

"It's personal."

Yes...all of it was personal.

Gratitude that seeing his face had helped her realize her misunderstanding.

She picked up her bag and stood.

As she went toward the coach, Ix cautioned, "Don't break it again."

"But you have replacement core material, yes?"

"Hey, that was for my wish. Next time, I'll be asking for a real repair fee from you. There's no more of that material in the world. Not even sure a country's entire treasury would be enough..."

"So stingy."

"I'm still just an apprentice."

"All right, I won't forget it."

The coach driver came to take her luggage. She handed it over and waited for the other passengers to board before her.

In a quiet voice, Ix added, "But I was able to get it because of you."

"What?" She turned toward him.

"Maintenance."

"Huh...?"

Ix hid his mouth with his hand and said, "I'm saying I'll do maintenance on the wand. You'll probably use the heck out of it at school, right? Come back to my shop anytime I'm in town, and I'll do it for cheap."

It took Yuui a moment to realize what he was trying to say.

Did that mean...?

She let out a huge sigh.

They did such delicate work...

So why were these craftsmen always so...?

"You are so clumsy, it's maddening," she reproached.

"What are you trying to say?" he asked, totally confused.

Yuui ignored him and boarded the coach.

Then she turned back to him, where he'd frozen to the spot, and asked, "Are you aware how expensive it is to travel from the Academy to this town?"

"...Very?"

"The opposite."

"Hmm?"

"Students of the Academy can use transportation for almost nothing."

Yuui closed the door without waiting for a reply.

She desperately tried to hide her smile under her hood.

©Enji

○

The boy picked up the stone.

It was red and shiny, and it felt warm to the touch.

He'd found it in the town square. It had fallen on the mound of sand that lay in its center. No, *fallen* wasn't the right word for it. Just as he'd been about to pass in front of the sand mound, the stone had appeared.

He'd looked to the sky but had seen no birds flying by. It wasn't as if anyone had thrown it, either. Besides, no one would ever toss out such a pretty gem.

So the boy had picked it up.

He didn't tell anyone about it. He carried it around like a good luck charm.

The boy didn't have parents. No one knew who his dad was, and his mom had died giving birth to him. Since then, it had always been just him and Grandma.

She called him names and had struck him on more than one occasion.

It wasn't just his grandma. Adults and children called him names and beat him. He didn't know how to fight back. All he could do was endure the pain and spend his days running from them.

And each time he did that, he saw the mountain.

The peak was easy to see from his bedroom window, towering over the town.

It always seemed so godlike to him.

So why did no one stop to notice?

There was nothing more fun than gazing up at it.

On windy nights, rainy nights, nights full of moonlight, and nights with a new moon, the boy considered the mountain.

And he spoke to it, within his heart.

He told it what happened each day.

What he liked.

What he hated.

He said he wanted to be stronger as tears streamed down his face.

He cursed them all, loathed them all.

And the mountain just towered over him, accepting his words.

Every night, after night, after night...

That was the boy's only salvation.

Which was why he started to think:

Perhaps this stone was something the mountain had given him.

He knew it was a pathetic daydream.

But the strange thing was, when he held on to it, he felt courageous.

Maybe it was only in his mind...

The boy changed. Just a little.

If they hit him, he struck back. If they called him names, he spat insults in kind.

That didn't end his torment, but it was indeed the birth of his pride.

Yet.

On that night, he stared up at the mountain as well.

The moon was nowhere to be found.

Thick clouds hid the sky, so it was pitch-black outside.

And yet the boy still stared.

He felt the warmth of the stone in his fist.

"...Huh?"

He tilted his head.

He thought he'd seen the mountain glow for just a moment.

He rubbed his eyes and stared again.

They weren't deceiving him.

Shimmering golden particles burst from the mountain's peak.

They climbed into the sky, illuminating the underside of the black clouds.

The heavens gleamed with stars.

As he took them all in, he forgot to breathe.

Dazzling light spread to fill the firmament.

So beautiful.

He'd never witnessed anything more beautiful.

The town continued to slumber.

The few people who were awake weren't looking at the mountain.

Save for just the one.

Only that boy saw the star-filled sky.

Eventually, the particles lost their sparkle.

The gold light faded.

The boy continued to stare at the night sky, which was once again cloaked in darkness.

He was about to cry, which seemed odd.

Why...?

He was neither sad nor in pain...

He felt such joy...

The miraculous night spoke of an end, with only a single tear as compensation.

Mount Agnas never rumbled again.

Afterword

Every reader has the liberty to decide where they'll start reading and where they'll stop. However, just as stories are rarely constructed with the assumption that the reader will begin at the end, I write this afterword with the presumption that it will be read last (I don't mean to imply there will be crucial spoilers here, but some may feel otherwise). Please understand.

This novel is based on *Dragon and Festival: From a Wandmaker's Perspective*, which received an honorable mention at the 11th GA Bunko Awards. Besides some rewriting and editing, the biggest difference between this book and the manuscript I applied with is, of course, the inclusion of Enji's incredible illustrations.

I wrote the first manuscript in January 2018, and I remember it taking me about two or three weeks to complete. Just now, I realize that was already a year ago. That's so long ago, in fact, that I really don't remember much of what I penned. Reading over it, I felt like I was reading someone else's work and kept asking myself, "*I* wrote this?" When they contacted me about the contest, I was locked in a battle to the death with Genichiro Ashina at the castle tower, and now I'm devoting myself to rebuilding the United States. In that way, too, I can feel the passing of the months and days.

I composed this story almost entirely in my room, but somehow, the night I finished writing, there was a sudden blackout, which shocked me. Not long after that, a brilliant light started to shine through my curtains. Thinking it strange, I opened them to find a nearly sixteen-foot-tall angler fish staring back at me.

"It's not dark now, is it?" said the angler fish.

"Isn't that to lure prey?" I inquired.

"It's case by case. I can change how I use it depending on the situation," he told me, which was reassuring. "Look up at the water's surface."

I did as he said and was surprised to see the surface of the water glowing red, almost as though it were on fire. It must have been a fairly strong light to have made it all the way down here in the ocean.

"What is that?" I asked.

"We're disposing of the overproduced light," replied the angler fish. "Last year, we set the light to be two percent stronger than shadow. Unfortunately, the person in charge of it last year failed to pass the baton properly, so the same settings have carried over to the current year."

"I see—so you're equalizing them."

"No, we actually plan to prioritize shadow by one percent this year."

The angler fish's job was to adjust the amount of light on the ocean floor. Normally, he wouldn't have anything to do with the light on the surface, but apparently, they were short-staffed, so they asked him to lend a hand. That kind of thing happens all the time.

I waited there until he finished the disposal.

Thankfully, my room was completely sealed, so no seawater leaked in, but I worried that the water pressure would crush my room at any moment. After this whole fiasco ended, I heard that some dumbo octopuses were kind enough to support the walls from the outside. It's really unfortunate I wasn't able to speak with them directly.

After some time, the ocean floor tour boat, the *Giant Oarfish*, came around and picked up my room. It was massive, over half a mile long, and the melancholy generator's low rumbling was oppressive. Of course, I wasn't the only passenger, so after they took me on board, I had to return home via the Aleutian Islands. The inside of the ship was just as opulent as people say it is. There was a reverse thousand-person bath made of Japanese cypress, a seven-hundred-square-foot backgammon board, and a special live performance by the Purple Albatrosses. I thoroughly enjoyed my time there.

While doing all that, I hit it off with another passenger named Murase, and they would sometimes sit beside me. Murase gave me a bottle of lemon-flavored Ramune when I left, but it feels like I would lose a precious memory if I drank it, so I haven't been able to bring myself to do it.

Once I returned home, I found a tree growing where my room used to be, which was a bit of an inconvenience. I felt bad chopping it down, so I decided to cut a hole in the floor of my room and raise the tree. Then I picked a cacao bean from it, which I then made into a chair—the very same one I am sitting on as I compose this afterword.

So unlike in reality where all sorts of things happen (such as being asked to write a four-page afterword even though you have nothing to write about), the various things in a narrative must be presented in a coherent manner. You have to show the characters, the setting, and parts of the plot, all while transitioning smoothly between them.

But with this novel, I somewhat narrowed the field of what I would actually depict. I decided that would be more sincere, considering the themes I was dealing with, and of course, just better overall. There may be some readers who finish this book and find some things unclear. That is intentional.

We have our two protagonists, our hero and heroine, and the story mostly advances through their points of view. The genre (not that there's any real point in defining it) would most likely be fantasy. There are many terms and a setting made specially for this work. The question is, Who or what does this story, told through the medium of an entire novel, revolve around? This in itself isn't the theme, but it is a thread that directly outlines the theme.

At the time of writing this afterword, preparations for Volume 2 are underway, but we'll see how that goes. There is still so much that is uncertain.

December 2019, Ichimei Tsukushi